Books by Ed Dunlop

The Terrestria Chronicles
The Sword, the Ring, and the Parchment
The Quest for Seven Castles
The Search for Everyman
The Crown of Kuros
The Dragon's Egg
The Golden Lamps
The Great War

Tales from Terrestria
The Quest for Thunder Mountain
The Golden Dagger

Jed Cartwright Adventure Series
The Midnight Escape
The Lost Gold Mine
The Comanche Raiders
The Lighthouse Mystery
The Desperate Slave
The Midnight Rustlers

The Young Refugees Series
Escape to Liechtenstein
The Search for the Silver Eagle
The Incredible Rescues

Sherlock Jones Detective Series
Sherlock Jones and the Assassination Plot
Sherlock Jones and the Willoughby Bank Robbery
Sherlock Jones and the Missing Diamond
Sherlock Jones and the Phantom Airplane
Sherlock Jones and the Hidden Coins
Sherlock Jones and the Odyssey Mystery

The 1,000-Mile Journey

TALES FROM TERRESTRIA: BOOK TWO

An allegory
by Ed Dunlop

cross & crown
PUBLISHING
RINGGOLD, GEORGIA

www.dunlopministries.com
Cover Art by Rebecca Douglas

The Golden Dagger : an allegory / by Ed Dunlop.
Dunlop, Ed.
[Ringgold, Ga.] : Cross and Crown Publishing, c2008
207 p. ; 22 cm.
Tales from Terrestria Bk. 2
Dewey Call # 813.54
ISBN 978-0-9817728-7-5

9817728-7-0

When two young goatherds witness the capture of a young horseman by enemy knights, they determine to help him, not knowing his identity or the incredible secret he is carrying.

Dunlop, Ed.
Middle ages juvenile fiction.
Christian life juvenile fiction.
Allegories.
Fantasy

Printed and bound in the United States of America

That my heart
would learn to trust
in the guidance of my King

Trust in the Lord
with all thine heart
and lean not unto thine
own understanding.
In all thy ways
acknowledge him,
and he shall direct thy paths.

–Proverbs 3:5, 6

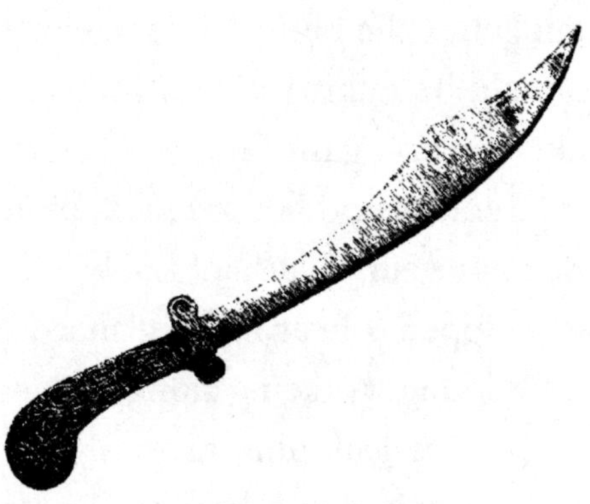

Chapter One

The afternoon wind howled in the treetops. It seized fistfuls of colorful autumn leaves, hurled them to the ground, and then threw them into the air again, spinning them about and making them pirouette in tight circles. Like a capricious child, the wind darted down to the river, set the reeds along the riverbank to dancing in unison, and then leaped upward to send fleecy clouds racing across the pewter gray sky.

High on the hillside overlooking Windstone Castle, two young goatherds, a boy and a girl, struggled against the wind as they rounded up a scraggly herd of Berkshire goats. The wind shrieked and howled, tugging at their thin clothing and spitefully throwing dust and debris in their faces. The afternoon was chilly and turning colder by the minute.

"Lanna!" fifteen-year-old Dathan called to his twin sister, "drive them toward me! If they get beyond the bluffs we'll never get them home."

"I'm trying, I'm trying," the girl answered impatiently, brushing a wisp of blonde hair away from her face. "Today these wretched animals have a mind of their own, don't they?" She darted forward to intercept a young goat that was determined to make an escape.

"Don't let them get to the bluffs," Dathan called again.

"Maybe you should be talking to the goats instead of me," the girl shot back. "I'm doing my best—" The staccato of hoof beats caught her attention and her gaze fell upon the roadway at the base of the mountain. "Dathan! Look!"

Dathan's heart skipped a beat as he glanced downward to see a dozen mounted knights racing along the dusty road. The powerful warhorses were galloping furiously, necks straining against their bridles, their flying hooves throwing sand and dust behind them like puffs of smoke. The knights were riding hard.

Lanna hurried close to her brother, gripping his arm so tightly that her fingernails dug painfully into his bare flesh. "Karnivan soldiers!"

"What would the Karns be doing here?" Dathan muttered as he carefully pried her fingers loose. The goats were temporarily forgotten.

"Dathan, look!"

At that moment, a lone gray horse raced into the roadway from a hidden draw. The rider threw a hasty, desperate glance back at his pursuers and the twins could see that he was a youth about their age. Like an arrow from a longbow, the fiercely galloping horse shot ahead and began to pull away from the pursuing Karnivan knights. Shouted commands from the soldiers seemed to urge the galloping gray horse to even greater speed.

"He's going to make it!" Lanna exulted, clutching her hands together under her chin as she watched the desperate race. "He's got a faster horse."

Both young goatherds found themselves drawn to the desperate young rider, though they had no idea who he was or the urgency of his situation. If the Karnivans were after him,

Lanna and Dathan were for him. "Ride hard," Dathan coaxed. "You're going to make it! You can do it!"

At that moment, disaster struck. The gray stumbled and went down, throwing her young rider headlong in the dust. With cries of delight the Karnivan riders were upon him, turning their mounts in a deliberate attempt to trample him underfoot. Lanna screamed in horror.

It happened too quickly for the eye to follow. Somehow the youthful rider managed to roll to his feet, springing clear of the nearest thundering horse. In a superhuman effort he leaped upward, clearing the back of the next horse and knocking his rider from the saddle. To Dathan's utter amazement, the youth caught hold of the saddle and pulled himself across it.

"He's getting away!" Lanna cried. A look of delight spread across her face.

But alas, it was not to be. Just then another Karnivan soldier reined in close and leaped from his saddle. He knocked the youth from the galloping horse, bearing him to the ground. With cries of triumph the remaining Karnivan riders wheeled their mounts and circled back to surround the struggling figures on the ground.

Dathan groaned. "They'll kill him."

As Dathan and Lanna watched, the armored knight leaped atop the smaller figure of the youth, crushing him to the ground and pounding him furiously with a gauntleted fist. The mounted knights cheered.

The cheers died in their throats as their companion was abruptly hurled backwards. Scrambling to his feet, the desperate youth ducked beneath the closest horse and disappeared into the brush at the side of the road.

The sudden move caught the Karnivan soldiers off guard. For several long seconds they sat astride their horses, staring first at their companion in the middle of the roadway and then at the bushes where their quarry had vanished.

"Don't just sit there, you idiots!" cried the Karnivan captain. "After him!"

Several knights spurred their mounts forward while others dismounted and dashed into the bushes. Lanna was wide-eyed as she turned to Dathan. "He got away!"

"Not yet, he didn't," Dathan replied gravely. "He can't run far. He's right at the river's edge and there's no place to hide. And besides, there are so many of them. They'll find him."

The twins continued to watch the unfolding drama as they resumed the task of rounding up the goats. The Karnivan knights, all afoot now except for their captain, searched the area frantically. Spreading out in a search pattern, they swept across the riverbank, beating the bushes and searching the undergrowth, checking each thicket and windfall. But the fugitive had vanished like a phantom.

At last, the Karnivan captain called his men back. "Head for the castle, men," he ordered. "We'll lodge here for the night."

The cavalcade of Karnivan knights rode swiftly along the riverbank, crossed the massive stone bridge a bowshot downstream, and rode up the steep approach to the castle. Two knights led riderless horses.

"He got away!" Lanna exulted. "I don't know who he was, but I'm glad he got away."

"Two horses," Dathan muttered. "Why are there two horses without riders?"

"One belonged to the stranger they were chasing..." Lana began, but Dathan cut her off.

"I know, I know," he said shortly, without intending to be impatient. "But there were two..." He scanned the riverbank and in the tangles of a dense thicket saw just a flicker of motion and the glimmer of polished armor. "Lanna, look!" he whispered fiercely. "One knight is waiting in ambush!"

"What do you mean? Where?"

Dathan pointed. "There. In the thicket, just beyond that boulder."

Lanna spotted the shiny armor. "What is he doing?"

"The lad they were chasing didn't get away. He went to ground somewhere nearby. That knight is waiting for the fugitive to come out so that he can catch him."

Lanna's eyes grew wide. "If he doesn't see the knight, he'll get caught! Oh, Dathan, we have to warn him!" She took a deep breath and turned toward the river, but her brother clapped a hand over her mouth.

"Lanna! If you shout a warning that knight will kill us."

She pulled his hand from her mouth. "Well, someone has to do something," she retorted. "They'll kill him!"

"We're slaves, Lanna," he reminded her gently. "I don't know what's going on here, but if we interfere, the Karnivans will kill us without a second thought." Remembering the goats, he turned and saw to his amazement that the entire flock was gathered close around him as though eager to head back to the shed. "Come on, we had better get the flock home or Garven will kill us!"

The goats were placidly making their way down the trail toward the bridge when Lanna grabbed Dathan's arm. "Look! There's the boy!"

The young goatherds paused and watched as a head appeared in the middle of the river. The youth glanced upward at the forbidding castle walls towering above the riverbank and then began to swim back toward the closest bank. Dathan chuckled softly. "He was hiding under that snag at the sandbar," he said admiringly. "How in Terrestria did he make it to the sandbar without the Karns hearing or seeing him?"

Lanna's eyes were wide with worry. "Dathan, he doesn't know that the soldier is waiting for him. He's walking right into a trap! We have to warn him!"

"Lanna, we can't," her brother replied miserably. "We dare not say a word, or the Karns will kill us!"

"They'll kill him if they catch him," she asserted, and drew in a great, sobbing breath as if she were about to break into tears.

"There's nothing we can do, Lanna."

The wind howled and moaned. With a loud cracking, splintering sound, a huge branch broke free from a tall sycamore and crashed to the ground. The hillside lit up with a brilliant flash of white-hot lightning, followed an instant later by an ear-splitting crash of thunder. A few huge drops of rain spattered down, stinging when they struck bare flesh. "Come on," Dathan shouted above the clamor of the wind, "let's get the goats in."

"I have you, rogue!" a harsh voice snarled in triumph, and the twins turned toward the river bottom in time to see the Karnivan knight leap from his ambush with sword drawn. "Not another step, knave, or I'll run you through!" The hapless youth raised both hands to show that he was not resisting.

"They caught him after all," Lanna whimpered, and then began to weep. "Oh, Dathan, what will they do to him?"

Dathan didn't want to think about it. He turned away as the grinning knight led his young captive at sword point toward the castle. "Come on," he said gruffly to Lanna, "let's get the goats home."

The rain fell faster.

Garven was waiting just inside the door as Dathan and Lanna led the restless flock of goats into the shed for the night. "You're late, boy!" he snarled. The stablemaster was in a foul mood and he demonstrated this by giving Dathan a fierce clout on the shoulder with a dirty fist. "You should have had the goats in before the rain started."

Anger stirred in Lanna's heart at the mistreatment of her brother. "We hurried, sir," she declared, blinking to hold back tears of anger. "Why do you strike Dathan?"

Garven turned in a rage. "A slave girl dares to speak in such a manner?" he growled. "You'll learn to hold your tongue, lass, or rue the day you were born." Open-handed, he slapped her across the face.

Dathan reached for a hay rake, but Lanna saw it. Sobbing, she grabbed his arm. "Dathan, don't," she whispered fiercely. "You'll only make things worse for both of us."

Her brother let out his breath through clenched teeth. Knowing that she was right, he nodded and turned away, clenching and unclenching his fists in an effort to control his seething anger.

Garven saw it. "Oh, let him at me, lass," he jeered. "Lord Keidric would understand if I killed a slave who attacked me."

The stablemaster was a tall, thin man with unusually long, sinewy arms, a neck like a turtle, and huge hands and feet. Grayheaded with a bald spot in the middle, he was clean-shaven except for a huge, droopy gray mustache that writhed when he talked. Garven had never married and therefore had no family; and his mean disposition and quick temper caused the servants and residents of the castle to keep their distance. Even the castle knights avoided him.

Garven seemed to take delight in making life miserable for the twins. As slaves and stablehands, they were responsible directly to him, and he had developed a knack for creating the most unpleasant chores and assignments for both of them. He was always particularly cruel to Lanna, as he realized the anguish that caused Dathan.

"Come on, boy," he jeered again, "take up that hay rake! Come at me, lad. You want to—I can see it in your eyes." He laughed as Dathan turned away.

"Fork down some fodder for the goats," he ordered them both. "When that's done, the lass can muck out the horse stalls. Boy, I want you to get some salt and take it to the cattle pen."

His eyes seemed to light up as a sudden thought occurred. "You were late with the goats, and for that you'll both do without supper."

"But we haven't eaten since breakfast," Lanna protested, and Dathan knew that she was close to tears. "Please..."

But the tall stablemaster only laughed. He raised a long, bony hand as if to strike her again. "Would you care to say more, lass?"

Lanna shook her head fearfully.

"I thought not."

An hour later, Lanna had finished mucking out the stalls. Exhausted and hungry, she stepped from the stables and stumbled across the castle bailey for a breath of fresh air. The sun had dropped behind the castle walls and the courtyard was shrouded in purple shadows. Night was almost upon them. *Why does he always make us muck out the stalls at night when the horses are in from paddock?* she thought wearily. *We could do it during the daytime without having to move the horses, but no...*

She sat down on the edge of the castle well. Feeling a gentle hand on her shoulder, she looked up to see Dathan standing over her. "Are you all right, Lanna?"

For his sake she struggled to hold back the tears. Not trusting herself to speak, she only nodded.

"I—I don't know why Garven has to be so cruel," Dathan said, and his voice trembled. Lanna looked up in surprise as she realized that he was struggling with his own emotions. "We both give him our best—we really do. And tonight...tonight I'm so hungry I could eat a bear!" He paused, and she saw the flash of anger in his eyes. "Lanna, if you hadn't stopped me, I think I would have tried to kill him."

She reached out and took his hand. "If only Papa was here..."

Footsteps sounded in the darkness, and they both looked up to see the tall figure of their tormentor approaching. "Head for the garde-robe," he ordered, referring to the primitive privy located at the top of the castle wall, "and then get to the loft and get some sleep. Tomorrow you'll both have a long day ahead of you, I warrant."

A female servant bearing a lamp and a bowl of food passed by just then, and the smell of the hot lamp and the tantalizing aroma of food engulfed them. Dathan swallowed and licked his lips. He and Lanna exchanged glances and Dathan saw the hungry, desperate look in her eyes.

He was not the only one. An evil grin spread slowly across Garven's long face and he called to the servant, "You there! Where are you going with those vittles?"

The woman paused just long enough to answer, "There's a young prisoner in the dungeon tonight. I suppose this is his last meal, for there's talk of hanging him at daybreak."

The woman turned away, but Garven called her back. "Come here, woman."

The servant approached fearfully. "Aye?" Her hands trembled and her face was filled with fear.

"Who talks of hanging the prisoner?"

"There's a cavalcade of Karnivan knights staying in the castle tonight. It seems that they chased the prisoner halfway across Cheswold, and they finally caught him just outside the castle this evening. As I said, they're talking of hanging him at first light."

"Hanging him? What's he done?"

The woman shrugged. "It's not my affair. I'm just taking the lad his last meal."

Graven waved his hand. "Give the meal to my stableboy here."

The woman frowned. "The prisoner is to be fed, sir—I have my orders."

"The boy hasn't eaten all day, woman. I'd daresay he's hungry, wouldn't you?"

The woman hesitated, not sure how to respond.

Dathan held his breath. *What is Garven up to? Is he actually going to feed me? And what about Lanna?*

"Woman, give the vittles to the boy."

Hesitantly, she complied, handing Dathan the simple meal. "But what about the prisoner?"

Garven laughed maliciously. "He'll get his food, my good woman. This lad is going to show his own temperance by taking the meal to the prisoner. He won't touch the food for he knows that I will kill him if he does. Right, boy?"

Dathan nodded helplessly. *So that's it! Knowing how hungry I am, he plans to torment me by making me take food to the prisoner.*

The stablemaster gave Dathan a stern look. "Get going, boy. But touch that food just once and there will be a double hanging at first light. Do you understand me?"

Dathan nodded miserably.

"Then don't just stand there like an idle wretch. Woman, give him the lamp."

Dathan took the lamp, and, turning toward the main gate of the castle, headed for the dungeon. He stepped forward into the tiny circle of light cast by the feeble glow of the lamp, not knowing that he had just taken the first step of a journey that was to change the future of the Northern Kingdoms of Terrestria.

Chapter Two

The lamp cast an eerie yellow glow on the damp stone walls as Dathan carefully made his way down a narrow set of decaying stone steps. The castle dungeon was a place that he had never seen, but he knew where it was located and he had found the corridor easily enough. He hesitated on the stairs, pausing just long enough to take a deep breath and attempt to calm his racing heart. The darkness was oppressive, almost terrifying, and the air was damp and reeked of death and decay.

I need to get out of here as fast as possible, he told himself, glancing nervously about at the ominous darkness. *I'll leave the food with the prisoner and hurry back to the stables as fast as I can go.*

The smell of the food was tantalizing, and he glanced down at it just once. *Turnip stew. If I took just one piece of turnip, it would never be missed. But Garven would somehow know about it. I don't think he'd kill me like he threatened, but he would beat me unmercifully.*

The stairs took a turn to the left, and with pounding heart Dathan followed them. The stench of rotting garbage was almost overwhelming and he tried to hold his breath as a defense against it. The stairs gave way to a narrow, low-ceiled corridor. At the foot of the stairs on a tiny bench sat a sleepy

Karnivan knight who wore no armor but was clad in leather leggings and a mail shirt. A short sword hung at his side. Above his head, a torch flickered feebly.

The soldier sprang to his feet at Dathan's approach and his hand went to the hilt of his sword. "What are you doing here, knave?" he demanded roughly. "No one is allowed down here."

"I—I brought food for the p-prisoner," Dathan stammered. He held the lamp close to the bowl so that the guard could see it. His hands trembled. This was the first time he had ever been this close to a Karnivan soldier, and he was terrified.

The guard stared at the food for several long seconds and then visibly relaxed. "Take it to him," he growled. "I'm going up for some air."

"Aye, sire," Dathan responded, with a long sigh of relief.

"I'll be at the top of the stairs, so don't try anything foolish."

"I—I wouldn't d-dream of it, sire. I'll just l-leave the food with the p-prisoner and be on my way."

"Stay until he finishes eating," the guard ordered. "I loathe turnips and I don't want the vessel left down here. Take it with you." With these words he turned and headed up the stairs.

"Aye, sire." Dathan moved toward the darkness of the narrow corridor. Terror swept over him in waves. The dungeon was nothing more than walls and stones and mortar, and he knew that; but it was a place of confinement, a prison, and the ominous atmosphere was oppressive. He struggled to breathe.

At the far end of the corridor his light fell upon a small grating in the wall secured by a sturdy iron lock. His heart pounded as he knelt and peered into the opening. The young rider that he and Lanna had seen on the roadway was seated against one dirt wall of a tiny enclosure less than two yards square. His knees were drawn up to his chin and his head rested on them in dejection and defeat. The ceiling of the cramped cell was barely a foot above his head.

Dathan stared in amazement. The tiny cell was less than four feet high. He studied the prisoner for a long moment, noting in surprise that the youth wore regal clothing. A dark doublet of elegant blue, deep crimson leggings, leather boots—this prisoner was of noble birth, perhaps even royalty. Dathan was awed by the sight.

"What are you staring at?" The words were sharp, demanding, and Dathan actually jumped in fright.

"N-nothing, sire," he said contritely. "I—I just brought you some vittles."

"Well, leave them and be about your business," the stranger growled. "Don't just stay there gawking at me as if I'm some sort of wild animal in a cage."

"I'm sorry, sire," Dathan replied quietly. Tipping the bowl slightly, he carefully slid it between the bars. "I was ordered to stay until you have finished."

Two strong hands reached for the dish and the young goatherd noticed that they were browned by the sun, sturdy and strong-looking. *This fellow has spent some time outdoors,* he realized.

The prisoner ate quickly but quietly, and Dathan's observations were confirmed. In the dim light he still hadn't seen the prisoner's face, but he could tell that this was a youth of high breeding. The prisoner paused for a moment. "Forgive my rudeness," he said quietly. "This has been a hard day, and I fear that I have abandoned my manners."

"Aye, think nothing of it," Dathan replied. He hesitated. "My sister and I saw your capture this afternoon," he ventured.

"We wanted to warn you, but we didn't dare. The Karns would have killed us."

"I am grateful for your sympathy, my friend, but there's really not much that you could have done." Dathan heard a long sigh. "So it ends this way."

"Why were they chasing you?" Dathan asked. "What have you done?"

The prisoner gave a low laugh, but it was not one of amusement or mirth. "It's a long story, my friend."

Boldness seized Dathan. "Will they really hang you in the morning?"

"Perhaps." The answer was forthright and direct, and Dathan could not detect the slightest trace of fear. He was amazed. "They'll either kill me or take me to Lord Grimlor. One is hardly worse than the other."

"Lord Grimlor?"

"The tyrant who seeks to take over the kingdoms of Northern Terrestria. Surely you know of him."

"A little. We have heard that he is evil."

"Evil is hardly the word for it," came the reply. "Grimlor is evil personified. One would think that he is the son of Argamor himself."

"What would he—Lord Grimlor—want with you?"

The youthful prisoner paused as he considered the question. At last, he spoke. "My name is Sterling, by the way." To the young goatherd's surprise, he actually extended his hand to Dathan.

As Dathan took the hand he found himself looking into a cheerful, friendly face. Dark, curly hair framed a bronzed face with lively eyes and a broad smile. "I—I'm Dathan," he stammered. "My sister Lanna and I are the goatherds for the castle."

"It's a delight to meet you, Dathan," Sterling said.

Dathan stared at him. Obviously, the youth was nobility, perhaps even royalty, yet he sounded as if he really meant it. "And I am glad to meet you, sire," Dathan replied.

Sterling laughed. "Drop the 'sire,' if you please," he requested. "You and I are almost the same age."

Abruptly, he grew sober. "You asked what I have done to arouse Lord Grimlor's interest in me," he said. "How much do you know about Grimlor and the Karnivans?" He took another bite of the turnip stew.

"I know that he is the ruler of Karniva," Dathan replied, "and that he is trying to claim Cheswold for himself. I know that the Karnivans are cruel, warlike people and that they are feared throughout the shires of Cheswold."

"Do you know that Grimlor is attempting to make Cheswold part of Karniva?"

"Aye."

"What do you know of Grimlor's hatred toward the Judan people?"

"I have heard that he has killed many, though I do not know why."

Sterling sighed. He passed the empty stoneware bowl through the bars to Dathan. "If you know the history of Terrestria, then you know that King Emmanuel himself was born of Judan ancestry. Grimlor hates the Judans for that very reason and has sworn to kill every last one of us—of them, I mean."

Dathan studied his face. "But what does that have to do with you?"

Sterling hesitated. "I am Judan."

The Karnivan guard entered the corridor at that moment. "Is the prisoner finished? I gave him more than enough time to eat."

Dathan seized the dish and leaped to his feet. "Aye, sire, he has finished."

As the young goatherd attempted to squeeze past the Karnivan knight in the narrow corridor, the guard gave a long yawn and rubbed his eyes wearily. "I hate to even think of standing watch tonight," he grumbled. "I ride hard on a manhunt all day and what reward do I get—I have to stand guard for six long, miserable hours! This is going to be one long, dreary night."

"Aye, sire, I'm sure it will be, sire," Dathan said politely, terrified to be in such close proximity to a Karnivan. His heart pounded furiously as he slipped past the man. In spite of his fear, he heard the clink of metal against the cold stone floor as he passed.

"Oh, what a night this is going to be," the burly guard groaned again, rubbing his eyes and sinking back to his seat on the tiny bench.

Dathan turned away, and in that moment, his heart leaped. Turning back for the briefest instant, he stole a furtive glance at the floor. In the blackness of the dungeon corridor, his eyes had not deceived him. On the floor lay a large iron ring with three keys on it.

One was the key to Sterling's cell.

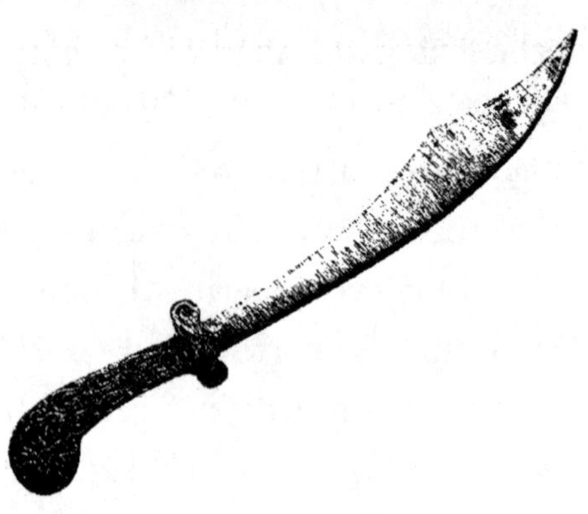

Chapter Three

Dathan's mind was in turmoil as he hurried across the darkness of the castle bailey. He couldn't get the image of Sterling's face out of his memory. Unless someone intervened, the friendly young prisoner would be hung at first light. Or perhaps even worse, taken to Karniva and turned over to Lord Grimlor. Dathan shuddered. Either prospect was terrifying.

He could still see the image of the dungeon keys lying in the darkness of the corridor. *If only I could sneak back into the dungeon and use those keys to free Sterling,* he thought wistfully. *I would actually be saving his life!*

The idea struck him like an arrow from a longbow. *What if I could really do it? What if I could somehow sneak back down those stairs, get the guard's keys, and...* He shook his head to clear his thoughts. His imagination was running away with him, and that could only lead to trouble.

But Sterling will die tomorrow morning, he reminded himself, *or at best, be taken to Karniva and turned over to Lord Grimlor to be killed.* His thoughts turned to the evil warlord. *Why does he hate the Judan people so?* he wondered. *Even if King Emmanuel himself was Judan, why would Grimlor hate the Judans so?*

"What are you doing, lad?" The gruff words cut through the

stillness of the night like the stroke of a sword, causing Dathan to jump in fright and drop the stoneware vessel. It shattered on the flagstones.

"I—I was t-taking food to the prisoner, s-sir," Dathan stammered.

The strong hand of the sentry gripped his chin, lifting his face so that his features were visible in the moonlight. "Taking food, were you?"

"Aye."

"By whose orders? You're a stableboy, are you not?"

"Aye, sir. Garven sent me, sir."

"Why would a stableboy be taking food to the dungeon? That's not your job, lad."

"G-Garven ordered me, sir."

The sentry thought it through. He glanced down at the shattered vessel. "I see. Well, hasten back to the stables. You should not be wandering the bailey at night."

"May I go to the garde-robe, sir?"

The sentry sighed. "Aye. Make it quick."

"Thank you, sir. Good night, sir." The sentry had already disappeared into the shadows of the night.

Moments later Dathan entered the stables and climbed the narrow ladder leading to the loft that he and Lanna shared with several other slaves. Tonight he was thankful that his sleeping spot was close to the ladder. Getting to bed would be much harder if he had to step over sleeping bodies.

With a grateful sigh he sank into the hay and closed his eyes. He was hungry, ravenously so, but tonight he was exhausted and sleep would come quickly. He yawned. *What will happen to Sterling?*

"Dathan!" Lanna's whisper jolted him awake.

"What?"

"What will they do to that young prisoner?"

"Sterling?" He sighed. "They will probably hang him, Lanna. Either that or send him to Karniva to be killed by Lord Grimlor."

"But why? What has he done?"

"He's Judan, Lanna. Grimlor and the Karnivans hate the Judan people and are trying to kill them all."

"How do you know he's Judan?"

"I talked with him. His name is Sterling, and he's Judan."

"Sterling." She said the name aloud, softly, as if trying out the sound of it. "That's a beautiful name."

Dathan was silent.

"I wish there was some way to set him free. He's about our age, isn't he?"

Dathan sighed. "I'd say he's almost exactly our age."

"But they're going to hang him." There was a tremor in her voice. "Unless someone can do something, they're going to hang him."

Dathan told her about his visit to the dungeon. Hesitantly, he told her about the keys on the floor.

She sat up. "You have to go back."

"What?"

"Dathan, you have to! Sterling will die at first light tomorrow! You have to go back!"

"Lanna, are you out of your mind? There's a Karnivan soldier on guard duty. He'd kill me if I tried anything."

"Then I'll go."

"Lanna..."

"Someone has to do something! If you won't go, I will."

"Lanna, listen to me!" Dathan whispered fiercely.

"Quiet down over there!" a grumpy voice demanded from across the loft. "We're trying to get some sleep!"

Dathan scooted closer to Lanna and placed his lips right against her ear. "Lanna, you don't know what you're saying. If we try to free Sterling from the dungeon, we'll be killed. The Karnivans apparently chased Sterling all day before capturing him. They're not going to take kindly to us if we try to set him free."

"And he's going to be killed if we don't." Lanna's lips were just inches from his face.

"I'm telling you—it would be impossible to get him out."

"We have to try. If you don't, I will."

"You haven't even been there. I have."

"Then you're the one who should go, aren't you?"

Dathan sighed and moved closer. "Listen to me. Even if we could get Sterling out tonight, the Karns are going to discover the escape at first light tomorrow, and right away they're going to know who did it. Who are they going to come for? Me! And they'll probably kill you, too."

"Then we'll run away with him," Lanna replied.

"You know what happens to runaway slaves," her brother retorted. "The penalty for running away is death."

Dathan's heart was in his throat as he crept silently down the narrow stairs toward the dungeon. The stairway was so dark that he could see nothing; he had to feel his way along. Step by step, slowly, carefully, he made his way down through the darkness. Fear gripped him, squeezing him so tightly that he could scarcely breathe. His heart pounded furiously. He felt dizzy and nauseous and he trembled in every limb.

I wouldn't even be here if Lanna hadn't insisted, he thought regretfully. *I shouldn't have listened to her.*

He paused after the first few stairs, leaning against the wall and struggling to catch his breath. If the Karnivan guard should hear him... Taking several deep breaths to calm himself, he again crept forward and downward.

When he turned the corner, the stench of rotting matter hit him in the face like a fist. He reeled, losing his balance and nearly tumbling forward. Gripping the wall with trembling hands, he tried to regain his composure. *I've been down these stairs before,* he told himself, *and I can do it again.*

But what if the guard hears me? Panic rose, threatening to overwhelm him. He struggled against it, pushing it back by the sheer force of his determination, and willing himself to continue.

A loud, rumbling roar suddenly filled the stairwell, and he cried out in alarm. He turned to run, but his legs gave way beneath him and he collapsed on the stairs, helpless to flee, helpless to fight. Terror overwhelmed him. There was a moment of rigid silence, and then the loud, rumbling roar again. Relief swept over him, sweet and refreshing in its intensity, and in spite of the perilous situation he had to laugh out loud. The Karnivan guard was snoring!

Reassured, Dathan crept forward with renewed zeal. Not only would the sound of the snoring cover any noise he made, it also told him that the knight was sound asleep. The Karnivan guard was the only real obstacle between him and success, and as long as the guard slept, he posed no threat.

The sputtering torch cast its feeble light on the sleeping guard as Dathan paused at the corridor entrance. He watched the Karnivan knight for several long seconds to be sure that all was safe. The man's head was thrown back against the stone wall; his mouth was wide open; and his chest rose and fell rhythmically with each snore. *He looks so peaceful,* the youth thought gratefully.

Silently, he crept forward. *The keys! Where are they?*

He spotted the ring of keys and his heart sank. The guard had one foot planted squarely on the ring! *Well, that ends all hope of rescuing Sterling,* he thought ruefully. *I don't dare try to move his foot.*

Disappointed, he stepped back out of the circle of light. There was nothing left to do but return to the loft and tell Lanna that he had done his best, that rescue was simply impossible. He had tried and failed, and there was nothing more that could be done. If she was asleep when he returned, he would tell her in the morning. Lanna had always been a sound sleeper and it was no easy task to awaken her.

The next rumbling snore was so loud that it seemed to shake the dungeon.

Dathan smiled as he remembered various times that he had played tricks on his sister while she slept. More than once he had placed unusual objects in her hands while she slept and enjoyed her bewilderment when later she awoke to find herself holding a pine cone or a milk pail, or, one occasion, a live terrapin. She was such a sound sleeper that one could do almost anything without waking her.

He watched the Karnivan soldier for another long moment. What if the man was as sound a sleeper as Lanna? Would it be possible to move his foot and retrieve the keys? With Lanna it would have been easy, but with the guard he was not so sure. And if the man awoke, well...

Trembling, Dathan knelt beside the Karnivan knight's leg. He held his breath as he steadied himself with one hand and reached across the man's leg with the other for the key ring. He pulled gently, but the guard's foot was planted squarely on the ring, rendering it immobile. He took a deep breath and tried again, but with no success. The key ring refused to move.

Watching the guard's face intently, Dathan leaned forward and gripped the toe of the man's boot. Not daring to breathe, he pulled upward with a gentle, steady pressure. The boot lifted, and the ring was free!

Hardly able to believe his good fortune, Dathan released the boot and reached for the key ring. The snoring stopped abruptly and the boot came back down on the key ring. Dathan held his breath. Sweat trickled down his back.

The guard shifted position slightly and resumed snoring.

Dathan waited until the snoring had resumed its normal pattern and then tried again. He gently lifted the boot, freeing the ring. But when he released the boot it came down squarely on the ring again, pinning it firmly to the floor.

The trembling youth tried twice more, but each time the results were the same. He was exasperated. He only had one free hand to work with, and each time he raised the boot and released it, the boot came down firmly on the key ring before he could move it.

Thoroughly frustrated, he decided to try one more time. Moving slowly, carefully, he gently raised the boot and then pushed the toe outward. When he released the boot and reached for the key ring, the boot came down again, but this time, it was barely on the ring. Dathan let out a long sigh and tugged on the key ring. To his great satisfaction, it slid free of the boot!

Elated, Dathan closed his fingers around the keys to keep them from jingling as he lifted the ring from the floor. Giddy with success, the youth stood silently to his feet and grinned at the sleeping form on the bench.

To his great horror, the man's eyes flew open and he sat

upright. Dathan froze. The Karnivan guard stared at him for a long moment without speaking. Dathan's heart pounded with terror. His chest constricted and he couldn't breathe. The blood pounded in his head. His mind reeled. What should he do? Should he try to make a run for it? In his terror, he found that he couldn't even move.

To Dathan's astonishment, the guard licked his lips and abruptly closed his eyes, muttering to himself and settling back against the wall to continue his rest. Dathan held his breath. After another anxious moment or two, the snoring resumed.

Dathan sagged with relief and let out his breath in a long, trembling sigh. *I thought he saw me,* he thought weakly. *Maybe he wasn't really awake.* He took several deep, quiet breaths in an effort to still his pounding heart. Moving slowly and carefully, he stepped over the guard's legs and crept to the end of the corridor. He knelt at the door to Sterling's cell.

Pausing to ascertain that the Karnivan knight was indeed still asleep, he silently selected a key and tried to insert it into the lock. But the key refused to enter the lock and he quickly realized that it was not the right one.

The second key slid in easily when he tried it. He twisted the key in the lock, but it refused to turn. He twisted the key in the opposite direction, and to his immense satisfaction, heard a muffled click as the key turned easily. He pulled on the grating and it swung toward him. Success!

"Who are you?" Sterling's cautious whisper startled Dathan. "What do you want?"

"It's me, Dathan."

"What are you doing here?"

"I came to get you out."

"Get out of here!" Sterling whispered fiercely. "They'll kill you if they find you here."

"I'll leave if you come with me," Dathan replied with delight. "Your cell door is now open."

A hand reached out and felt along the edge of the floor and then reached over and touched the cell door. An exclamation of astonishment followed.

"Come on," Dathan urged. "The guard is asleep. Let's go." Just then a rumbling snore shook the dungeon.

Five minutes later, Dathan crouched over the sleeping form of his sister. He leaned forward until his mouth touched her ear. "Lanna, wake up!"

Lanna stirred and turned over on her side. Dathan shook her. She moaned softly and pulled away. "Lanna, wake up. Sterling is waiting and we have to go."

Dathan tried unsuccessfully for several more minutes to awaken his sister, but Lanna seemed determined to stay asleep. He shook her, whispered in her ear, and even tried opening her eyelids, but all to no avail. Somehow, his sister refused to be wakened.

Finally, Dathan resorted to a desperate measure. Pinching Lanna's nostrils shut with one hand, he covered her mouth with the other. For several long seconds, nothing happened. Suddenly Lanna seized his hands and tried to pull them away. He held on. Her eyes flew open and she struggled to sit up.

"Lanna, it's me!" he whispered urgently, and then released his grip. "Keep quiet!"

Lanna gulped huge lungfuls of air. "You tried to—"

He clapped one hand over her mouth. "Lanna, keep quiet! I freed Sterling from the dungeon. We have to leave without waking the others."

She nodded, and he knew that she was now awake. He took

his hand from her mouth. She was breathing hard. "Were you able to get to Sterling?"

"Aye. He's free," Dathan repeated in a whisper. "Come on, we're leaving the castle. Sterling is waiting for us."

Moments later, two shadowy figures crept furtively across the bailey until they came to the base of the inner castle curtain. "Sterling is going to meet us here," Dathan told Lanna.

Just then a rustling in the bushes gave away the location of Sterling's hiding place, and the twins ducked beneath the shrubbery and crawled to meet him. They found him waiting patiently at the very corner of the bailey. "Sterling, this is my sister, Lanna," Dathan greeted him.

"It's a pleasure to meet you, my lady, though I cannot see you properly," came Sterling's whispered greeting.

"And I am glad to meet you," replied Lanna simply.

"Lanna and I are going to come with you," Dathan announced.

"I don't think that's such a good idea," Sterling replied. "If the Karnivans capture me, I'm facing almost certain death. If you're caught with me, you would face the same fate."

"We can't stay here in the castle," Dathan reminded him. "We're responsible for your escape. How well do you think that's going to strike the Karns?"

The other youth hesitated. "You might as well know," he said at last. "I must travel all the way to the border of Ainranon. It is only there that I will find safety."

"Ainranon!" Dathan exclaimed. "But that's—"

"More than three hundred miles southeast of here," Sterling finished for him. "It's going to be one difficult journey."

"But you'd have to cross half of Cheswold and all of Karniva," Dathan remarked. "Would it not be better to head directly south into Carpia?"

"You know Terrestrian geography quite well for a servant," Sterling remarked.

"Lanna and I were not slaves until just recently," Dathan replied. "We'll tell you more about it when we have the time." He frowned. "But as I said, would it not be better to travel to Carpia?"

"Nay," the young Judan replied. "There are those who suspect that the king of Carpia is in league with Grimlor. If that is true, Carpia would be more dangerous than staying here in Cheswold. Nay, I must go to Ainranon and find Lord Stratford. He will take me to my father and safety—in Eastern Ainranon."

"But we must go with you!" Dathan insisted. "If you have to stay out of sight, you dare not ask for food and lodging. You need us! If we were to travel with you, we can help you."

Sterling shook his head. "I don't think you realize the dangers you would face."

"We have to leave the castle anyway," Lanna insisted. "We can't stay here."

"I thank you for helping me escape the dungeon," the youth said earnestly. "And I appreciate your willingness to risk your life for mine. But I must travel alone. In the morning I will sneak my horse from the stable and ride from the castle the moment they lower the drawbridge. I will travel far faster alone and on horseback than the three of us could travel together."

"You'll never get your horse out of the castle," Dathan told him.

"Why do you say that?"

"The stablemaster is a cruel man by the name of Garven," Dathan replied. "He's always up long before first light and he watches the stables like a hawk. No horse comes or goes without his knowing about it. You'd never get your horse past him."

"Could you get it for me?"

Dathan sighed. "Garven watches us as closely as anyone else. He doesn't trust us. If we touched your horse he'd be on us like a cat on a mouse. We wouldn't have any more of a chance than you would."

Sterling thought it through. "Then I will have to go afoot," he decided. "It would be far better to have my horse for I could travel faster and farther, but if I must go afoot, then I will."

"As long as Lanna and I are fleeing the castle," Dathan told him, "we might as well travel with you. We can help each other."

The young fugitive looked at Lanna. "And what about you, Lanna? Are you in agreement with your brother?"

Lanna shrugged. "I see no other way. As Dathan just pointed out, he and I are now fugitives. We might as well travel with you."

"But do you realize the dangers that you will face? You and Dathan would be safer traveling by yourselves rather than traveling with me. If we are captured by the Karnivans, we will all face certain death."

"We are willing to take that risk," Dathan interjected.

"Aye," the girl agreed, "we are willing."

Sterling was silent for a long moment. "Then it is settled," he said at last. "We will travel together to Ainranon."

"Let's leave immediately," Lanna suggested, "and get as far away from here as we can before daylight."

"We need to leave as soon as possible," Sterling agreed, "but the castle entrance is sealed until morning. The drawbridge is up, the portcullis is down, and the gates are barred—we have no way to get out of the castle."

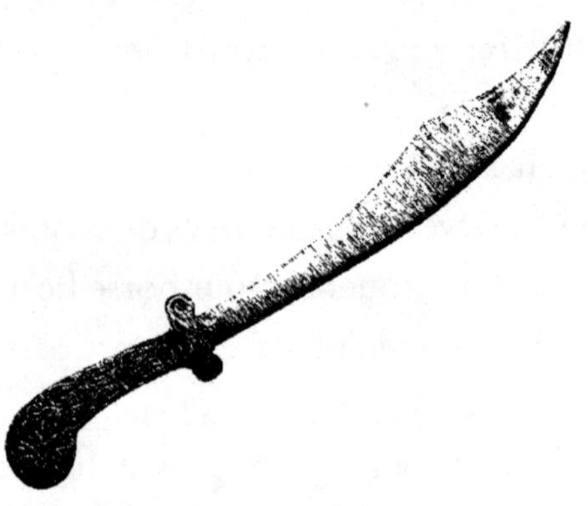

Chapter Four

The three young people sat hidden in the shrubbery in the north bailey of Windstone Castle as they pondered their predicament. "There's no way out of the castle," Sterling repeated. "The gates won't be opened until sunrise, and by then they will have discovered my escape."

He looked at Dathan. "Is there another way?"

"It's either over the wall or through the gate," Dathan replied. "That's the only two ways that I know of."

"What if we sneak up to the sentrywalk when the sentry is at the far end of the wall," Lanna suggested, "and then jump into the moat and swim across?"

"The outer curtain wall is thirty-some feet high," Sterling replied. "That's a long way to fall, even landing in water. And the sentries are sure to hear the splash of our landing. One arrow from a sentry's longbow, well... it's just too risky."

"Suppose we just wait here until they open the gates," Dathan suggested, "and then just walk out as if we're going on an errand."

"That will work if they haven't discovered my absence," Sterling replied. "Once they find out that I'm gone, they'll seal off the gates until I'm found or until they're convinced that

I'm nowhere in the castle."

"We can only hope that your absence is not discovered until after the castle gate is opened," Dathan said.

"Let's stay here and try to get some sleep," Sterling said. "As soon as they open the gates tomorrow morning we will attempt to walk out. It is a simple plan, but as far as I can see, it is our only plan."

"I hope it works."

"Good night, both of you," Sterling said quietly as the trio lay down beneath the shrubbery and tried to get comfortable. "Tomorrow will bring what it will bring."

As Dathan closed his eyes and tried to go to sleep, worry swept over him like a cold draft. Would they escape the castle safely? What would happen if the guards discovered Sterling's absence before the sentries opened the castle gates? At last, his restless thoughts subsided and he drifted off to sleep.

The shrill crowing of a rooster jolted Dathan awake. He sat up immediately, fully alert, and nearly in panic. *We've overslept!* he thought frantically. *We should have been up an hour ago!* He glanced over at Sterling and discovered to his chagrin that the spot was empty. Sterling was gone. Dathan seized his sister by the shoulders and shook her. "Lanna, wake up!" he whispered urgently. "Get up! We have to leave the castle as fast as possible—if we're not too late already!"

"Unh," Lanna groaned. She turned over and curled up, drawing her knees up to her chin as she attempted to stay asleep.

Dathan shook her again. "Lanna, wake up!"

His sister slept on.

Frantic now, Dathan crawled to the edge of the shrubbery to check the bailey for some indication that Sterling's escape had been detected. If the courtyard swarmed with Karnivan soldiers shouting orders and searching the castle grounds then he would know that their escape attempt was about to be thwarted. He paused in bewilderment. The bailey was dark. He glanced toward the heavens and saw that the skies above the castle were dark with the slightest hint of a faint glow in the east—sunrise was still at least half an hour away. Letting out his breath in a long sigh of relief, he sat back and relaxed. *It's not as late as I thought.*

Sensing movement beside him, he turned and then jumped in fright as a dark figure darted toward the bushes. His breath caught in his throat. One of the servant girls! Their hiding place had been discovered and their escape plan was about to end in failure. To his astonishment, the girl ran directly toward him, then dropped to her knees and rolled under the shrubbery, all in one quick motion. She lifted her head and looked directly at him.

Dathan took one look at the girl's face and then burst into laughter. The furtive figure was Sterling, dressed in the clothing of a servant girl! A dirty, tattered gown of faded homespun covered his regal clothing and on his head he wore what appeared to be a towel. "Sterling! What in Terrestria? I thought you were a servant girl—"

"If the sentries are looking for an escaped prisoner, perhaps this will fool them for a moment or two and at least get me past the gate," the youth explained with a shrug. "I found it in the trash heap behind the kitchen."

Reaching within the gown, he produced several items. "I also found these." Dathan leaned closer and saw a small loaf of bread and several apples. Sterling grinned at him. "Are you interested?"

"Aye!" Dathan replied eagerly. "Lanna and I haven't eaten since yesterday morning."

A hand touched Dathan on the shoulder and he turned to find Lanna right beside him. "What are we doing?"

"Sterling found us some food," he told her happily.

"First light is only twenty or thirty minutes away," Sterling told the twins. "Let's eat and get ready to go."

They were just finishing the last of the bread when a stern voice called from right beside their hiding place, "Unbar the gates! We have a hanging to attend to!"

"Aye, sire," the sentry called. "Right away, sire!" Within moments, the creak of hinges and the clatter of chains told the three fugitives that the gates were being opened and the portcullis was being raised simultaneously.

Sterling leaned forward. "Ready? Let's go!"

Stiff with fear, the three fugitives crawled from beneath the bushes and sauntered toward the inner curtain gate, trying to look as casual as possible. They passed through without incident, crossed the barbican, and approached the main gate. The massive oaken gates were now wide open and the portcullis was slowly going up. "Lower the drawbridge," Sterling muttered under his breath. "Come on, come on, lower the drawbridge."

Just then the drawbridge began to drop.

"Lord Keidric approaches the castle!" a sentry called.

Dathan glanced at Sterling. "Oh, no."

The Judan youth shrugged. "This could prove to be a blessing, my friend. This may give us the distraction that we need. Let's stay out of sight for another moment."

The trio slipped behind a myrtle tree in the barbican as the drawbridge continued to lower with the rattling of chains and the creaking of hinges.

Moments later a cavalcade of mounted knights rode through the gates and into the barbican. Clad in shining armor with pennants waving, they were an impressive sight. At the head of the procession rode a tall, broad-shouldered knight astride a magnificent white stallion. The knight was bare-headed and his blond hair seemed to glisten like spun gold. A well-trimmed beard gave him an aura of elegance.

Dathan ducked behind the tree. "Lord Keidric!"

The knights rode through the inner gate and entered the bailey. "Let's go," Sterling whispered.

Slipping from behind the tree, the trio hurried toward the main gate. Just as their feet touched the planks of the drawbridge, a shouted alarm echoed within the castle bailey. "The prisoner has escaped! Raise the drawbridge!"

Dathan and Lanna froze with fear. Almost immediately, the massive drawbridge started to go back up.

"Go!" Sterling cried. "Run for it!" He shoved them both forward to goad them into action and then dashed across the drawbridge. Dathan and Lanna were right on his heels. The end of the drawbridge was already more than two feet from the ground. The three fugitives leaped from the end to land safely in the roadway of the castle approach.

"Halt!" cried the voice of the sentry from the battlements of the outer curtain. "Halt, I say!"

Dathan hesitated.

"Don't stop!" Sterling cried. "Follow me!" He dashed forward, sprinting as hard as he could for the bridge spanning the river. Lanna and Dathan were right behind him.

"Lower the drawbridge!" cried a voice from within the castle. "Lower the drawbridge! Come on, you idiots, they're getting away!"

"Aye, sire! Sorry, sire!" came the contrite voice of one of the sentries.

Dathan glanced back. The drawbridge was already at a steep

angle and he knew that the horses couldn't cross it until it was lowered. *That will buy us some time,* he thought gratefully.

"Run, Dathan! Run Lanna!"

Trembling with fear, the trio of fugitives dashed frantically across the bridge and up the slope into the forest. The twins followed Sterling, thankful for the thick groves of boxwood and chestnut that partially concealed them from the castle. Their hearts pounded furiously. Their escape from the Karnivans had been too close, and all three realized that they were still in extreme danger.

Within moments Sterling found an old game trail and began to follow it, running at a pace that soon had the twins gasping for breath. After a furlong or two Lanna felt as if she could go no farther. "We have to rest," she declared, dropping to her knees in the middle of the trail.

But Sterling immediately grabbed her hand and pulled her to her feet. "Nay," he said urgently, "there is no time to rest! They are not far behind us! We have to go on!"

As if to back up his statement, at that moment a stern voice echoed through the trees, barking orders in Karnivan. The soldiers were indeed on their trail. Overcome with terror, the three fugitives ran until their lungs burned and their sides ached. When the trail crossed a little stream that tumbled along a rocky bed, Sterling hesitated for just an instant and then splashed into the water. "We must wade in the stream for a few furlongs," he told the others. "It will make our trail harder to follow."

They splashed into the stream. The current was swift but the water was shallow and they were in no danger of being swept off their feet. "Watch your step," Sterling cautioned. "If you slip you'll spend the rest of the day in wet clothing."

Sterling, Lanna, and Dathan followed the stream for four or five furlongs, wading through swift riffles and shallow pools, clambering over slippery, mossy rocks, and occasionally leaving the stream to traverse a pool that was too deep to wade. When the stream crossed a second game trail, Sterling left the stream and began to follow the trail.

"We have to rest," Lanna begged. "I can't keep going like this."

Sterling paused. They were entering a shady, secluded glen filled with large ferns. Splashes of sunlight filtered through the canopy of leaves overhead to create dappled patterns of light on a huge log that lay beside the trail. "All right," he conceded. "But just for a few moments."

Thoroughly spent, the trio sank to their knees in the middle of the trail, gasping for breath. Dathan's heart was pounding as if it wanted out of his chest. "I hope we've lost them," Lanna declared. "We can't run like this all day."

Sterling abruptly held up one hand. "Sh-h! Listen!"

The staccato of hoof beats echoed through the woods. "Quick!" Sterling cried, "behind the log!" He leaped to his feet and scrambled over the top of the log to drop into the ferns behind it. The twins were right behind him.

Seconds later, three mounted knights thundered into the glen, swept around a bend in the trail and disappeared from view. Dathan caught just a glimpse of the riders but there was no doubt as to their identity: they were Karnivans. He stood up. "That was close!"

Sterling grabbed him and dragged him down behind the log. "Lie still!"

Two more horsemen thundered through the glen and disappeared down the trail.

After waiting in silence for several more moments, Sterling rose quietly to his feet. "Let's leave the trail and work our way straight down the slope," he told the others. "If we follow the trail we take a greater chance of running into the Karnivans."

Dathan gave him an admiring glance. "How did you know that the second group of riders was coming? If you hadn't pulled me down, they would have seen me. I never even heard them coming!"

Sterling was nonchalant. "When you have been a fugitive as long as I, you will learn these things," he said simply. He pulled a compass from within his clothing and studied its face for a moment or two. "We need to head southeast," he told his companions. "The village of Cheskirk is only thirty miles from here. I figure we can make it in two days, although we are facing some of the most rugged country in all of Terrestria. We need to put as many miles as possible between us and the Karnivans."

He tucked the compass into a pocket and turned to Lanna. "Think you can hike for a while longer? We have to go on."

She nodded wearily.

The afternoon shadows were growing long as the three exhausted young people rested in the shade of a huge oak on a hillside overlooking a wide, peaceful valley. Dathan lay on his back on the mossy ground. "I am so tired," he groaned.

"But at least we're free," Sterling reminded him. "We're still ahead of the Karnivans."

At that moment the deep bass voice of a hound echoed across the hillside. A look of panic swept across Sterling's face, and Lanna saw it. "What is it?" she asked.

"It's what I feared the most," Sterling answered. "It's a Karnivan boar hound. They've put dogs on our trail."

Dathan rolled to his feet. "What can we do?" he asked.

"We'll have to move faster and do a better job of covering our tracks. The boar hounds are large, vicious dogs with great tracking abilities. The Karnivans love to hunt wild boars, and they use these dogs to track and corner the boars. As vicious as the boars are, one boar hound can hold several of them at bay until the hunters arrive for the kill."

Dathan was worried. "If they're on our trail then we're in trouble."

Sterling nodded. "Big trouble." He studied the terrain for a moment. "Let's stay in the forest until we reach that point where the valley narrows. We'll cross the valley at that point, maybe even follow the stream down. We have to do everything we can to confuse the trail for the dogs."

The youth took off at a dead run through the woods with the twins right behind him. "Stay with me," he called over his shoulder, "and do everything that I do. I'm going to try to leave a trail that will confuse the dogs."

Moments later when Sterling came to a small creek, he splashed up it for a hundred yards and then left the water to run in tight circles along the bank. Crossing the stream, he did the same on the opposite bank and the reentered the water and continued upstream. The twins did their best to keep up. Several hundred yards upstream, they came to a large eucalyptus tree that extended out over the water like a giant arm. Sterling pulled himself up into the branches and then ran along the horizontal trunk. Leaping into the branches of a nearby tree, he crossed to the opposite side and then dropped lightly to the ground more than ten yards from the stream. The twins followed.

For the next fifteen minutes, Sterling traveled at a dead run, laying the most confusing trail imaginable. Dathan and Lanna did their best to keep up as he doubled back on their trail time after time, laid false trails to one side or the other, and splashed in every stream they came to in an attempt to avoid leaving a scent for the dogs to follow. They ran along the top of fallen logs, crossed narrow ravines by swinging across on vines, and fought their way through brambles and thickets. They ran until their lungs burned and their sides ached, and yet the baying of the hounds came closer and closer.

"I've tried every trick I know and yet they're still gaining on us," Sterling panted wearily. "I really don't know what else to do."

Moments later, as the three fugitives worked their way down a steep, rock-strewn slope, they heard a strange snuffling, snorting sound and a heavy crashing in the bushes. Sterling spun around and seized a large rock in each hand. "We can't outrun them," he said, with resignation. "The dogs are upon us. Lanna, get behind us."

Following Sterling's lead, Dathan picked up two large rocks. Just then a large black and brown dog came bursting from the thickets. Spotting his quarry, he tensed, lowered his head, and began stalking toward them, growling and snarling as he came. Moments later a second dog ran from the bushes and joined his companion. Side by side, the two fierce dogs advanced slowly down the slope, teeth bared, their throats rumbling with angry snarls.

"So these are boar hounds," Dathan moaned. "We don't stand a chance against two of them."

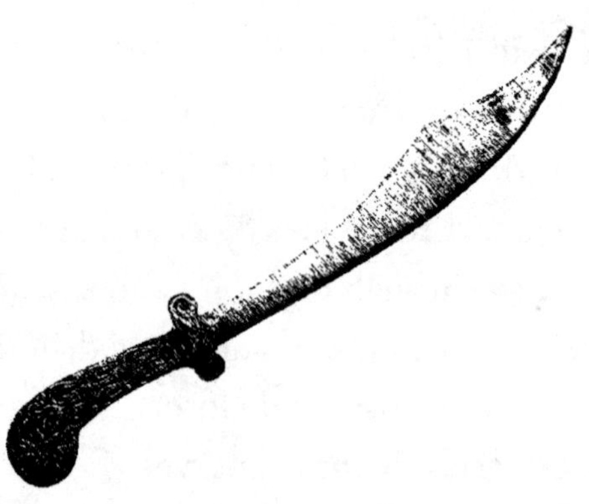

Chapter Five

Growling ominously, the two huge dogs crept down the rocky slope toward the three terrified fugitives. Heads low, ears laid back and teeth gleaming white, they acted as if they intended to eat their quarry alive.

Dathan's heart pounded with terror. Gripping the rocks with trembling hands, he slowly drew back his arm as he prepared to hurl the first missile. "W-Where-where are th-the K-Karnivans?" he quavered. "Th-These dogs are r-ready to k-kill us!"

"Wait until they get closer," Sterling instructed calmly, and Dathan glanced at him in surprise. "Don't throw until I say so."

The dogs moved in for the kill.

Lanna began to whimper. "Dathan, do something!"

"Steady," Sterling said softly. "Don't throw yet. Wait until they're closer."

As they approached, the boar hounds seemed to become more and more ferocious. Deep growls rumbled in their chests and slipped through bared teeth as angry snarls. Lowering their heads even further, they crept toward the terrified trio, opening and closing their jaws slightly as if in anticipation of a feast.

Dathan's heart constricted with terror and he found that he couldn't even move. "Sterling..."

"Don't move," came Sterling's whisper. "Just wait."

The dogs crept closer.

"Hold perfectly still," Sterling whispered.

Paralyzed with fear, Dathan struggled to draw a breath. He knew that his sister was as terrified as he.

"Stop!" Sterling commanded in a low voice.

The dogs froze, motionless, but the growling continued.

"Get back!" Sterling ordered in the same low, authoritative voice. He took half a step forward.

Both dogs flinched and then moved their shoulders back just a fraction of an inch. Growls rumbled in their throats.

"Get back!" Sterling repeated, louder and sterner this time. "Get back!" He took another half step toward the dogs.

To Dathan's astonishment, both dogs retreated a few inches. The growling was lower, less ferocious. Both tails were lowered a bit.

"We have them now," Sterling whispered. He took a full step in the dogs' direction. "Get back, I say!" he ordered.

Both dogs moved backward. Their heads and tails drooped. The growling stopped.

Turning his full attention to the animal on his left, Sterling pointed at the dog and snapped his fingers. "You! Lie down!" he ordered in a voice that carried authority.

To the astonishment of Lanna and Dathan, the cowed dog immediately lay down on the rocks. Slowly, tentatively, his tail began to wag.

Sterling turned on the other dog. "You," he ordered, pointing and snapping his fingers, "lie down!" Just as her companion had done, the second dog lay down and then slowly wagged her tail.

Dathan was astonished. "I don't believe this!" he exclaimed.

"Stay still and stay quiet," Sterling cautioned. "Please."

Moving slowly and cautiously, Sterling advanced toward the first dog. "Stay," he said quietly, but firmly. "Stay." Continuing to talk quietly but with a note of authority, the youth knelt in front of the boar hound. After several minutes, he slowly extended one hand and allowed the dog to sniff it. Leaning back away from the dog, he extended both hands and beckoned to the animal. "Come," he said softly.

To Dathan's amazement, the huge dog crawled forward until his muzzle was touching Sterling's knee. He allowed Sterling to reach out and touch him.

Sterling repeated the process with the other dog. Within minutes, both of the ferocious boar hounds were frisking around Sterling as if they belonged to him. "Keep your distance until they get to know me a little better," the youth suggested to Dathan and Lanna. "These hounds have outrun their masters, so we're taking them with us. Come on, we need to put some distance between us and the Karnivans."

Dathan shook his head and gave Sterling an admiring glance as they resumed their journey down the hillside. "That was the most amazing thing I have ever seen."

Sterling grinned. "My father always kept good hunting dogs," he said, "and I grew up around them. I speak their language."

"Aye, that you do," Lanna agreed.

"I think I'll name them Boris and Bortha," Sterling said.

"Which is which?" Lanna asked.

"Boris is the male; Bortha is the female," Sterling responded.

Late in the afternoon of the third day, the three exhausted young people lay on their bellies on a grassy knoll. Boris and Bortha lay on either side of Sterling. The trip had been hard. Berries, nuts, and a few edible roots that Sterling had found had been their only food, and the travelers were hungry, tired, and discouraged.

Just below them, a twenty-foot bluff bordered a small glen in which a lone oak and a mimosa tree stood proudly. The fern-like branches of the mimosa swayed in the afternoon breezes, beautiful and alluring. Sterling studied the glen. "Wild boars have been frequenting the glen for the acorns from the oak," he told his companions.

Dathan leaned over for a closer look. "How do you know?"

"You can see their tracks," the other replied. "They're all over the glen." Sitting up, he hefted the homemade spear that he had been sharpening for two days. "We must have food," he said. "Perhaps we should stay here tonight so that I can hunt the boars when they come to feed this evening."

"Wouldn't that be dangerous?" Lanna asked. "I've heard that wild boars are vicious."

Sterling nodded. "They can be," he agreed. "But I could hunt them here in the glen with no danger whatsoever."

"How would you do it?" Dathan asked.

"From the mimosa," Sterling replied. "See that one branch down low? I could lie on that and spear any boar that passed under that branch."

"What if they didn't pass under the branch?"

"That's where Boris and Bortha would come in. I would simply have them drive the boars beneath that branch and then I would choose the boar I wanted."

"Would they do that?"

Sterling petted Boris, grabbing his ears and twisting them affectionately. "I'm sure they would. They're boar hounds, aren't they? And we've all seen in the last couple of days how intelligent they are. I'm sure they were well-trained in hunting techniques by the Karnivans."

"When would the boars come?"

"Typically just before sundown."

Dathan shrugged. "Then perhaps we should wait until sundown. We haven't seen any sign of the Karns for two days now."

"They gave up when their dogs disappeared," Lanna suggested.

Sterling laughed. "Perhaps. But we have to be on our guard. We can't assume that the Karnivans have abandoned the chase. We still have to be alert."

"Why are the Karns after you?" Dathan asked.

Sterling shrugged. "As I have told you, I am Judan. Grimlor and the Karnivans have sworn that they will slaughter every Judan in Terrestria."

"But there were a dozen of them chasing you," Dathan argued. "Twelve knights after one youth...?"

The other gave a wry smile. "They were determined to catch me, I assure you of that."

"But why? Why would twelve armed knights chase one unarmed youth?"

"Well, now it's five against twelve," Lanna spoke up. "Boris and Bortha have joined our side, haven't you?" Raising up on her knees, she tousled Bortha's fur. The big dog responded by leaning her head to one side and letting her tongue hang out as if she thoroughly enjoyed the attention.

Dathan looked thoughtfully at the two boar hounds. "Where did Boris and Bortha come from?"

Sterling glanced at him. "What do you mean?"

"When Lanna and I saw the Karns chasing you by our castle, they didn't have dogs with them. So where did the dogs come from?"

"I don't know."

Dathan looked Sterling in the eye. "Tell me the truth, friend—are there other companies of Karn soldiers chasing you?"

Sterling looked uncomfortable. "I really don't know how many Karnivans are pursuing us," he replied. "And that's the truth."

Dathan thought it through. "But there are more than twelve."

"Perhaps. I do not know how many there are."

Dathan looked at the spear which Sterling had made by sharpening the point of a branch and hardening it in a small, smokeless fire. "So you really think you could kill a wild boar with that?"

"Oh, I know I could. My father and I have hunted wild boar before."

He looked at Lanna and Dathan. "I've only known you a few days, but I can tell that you have not been slaves long. Would you care to tell me your story?"

"We have only been at the Windstone Castle a few weeks," Dathan said, nodding. "We came from the shires in western Cheswold."

"Papa is not a landowner, but he is a master craftsman," Lanna said proudly. "He is a carpenter."

"So why were you sold into slavery?"

"Papa had debts that he could not pay," the girl replied, "and we were sold to pay his debts."

"Your own father sold you?"

"Nay, Papa would never do that," Dathan interrupted. "Papa's creditors came and took us. Papa had no choice."

"And so you were sold to Sir Keidric."

"Aye," the twins replied, nodding.

"What kind of a man is he?"

Dathan shrugged. "We've only seen him once before. We saw him for the second time when he came through the gate the other morning. We really don't know him and he doesn't know us. We work for the stablemaster, Garven. And he's meaner than a she-bear with cubs."

Sterling nodded. "I would assume he's a reflection of his master, Sir Keidric." A faraway look came into his eyes. "You know, I had a strange dream last night. I dreamed that I was a little boy again, and that I was fishing in the moat at Windstone Castle! There was a really big man fishing with me, and..."

"Sterling, look!" Dathan exclaimed quietly, pointing into the glen below. "Your wild boars are here!" As he spoke, three wild boars came trotting into the glen, snorting and growling and popping their teeth as if they were in a foul mood. They began to root beneath the trees for acorns.

"They look mean," Lanna remarked, shivering with fear. "Look at their teeth."

"Those tusks can rip a man open in an instant," Sterling told her. "The wild boar is very dangerous animal."

"Are you sure you want to tackle one of these?" Dathan asked. "I'd sure hate to have them come after me."

"We need food," Sterling replied. "I'll hunt from the tree, so I'll be all right."

"Well, be careful."

"I should have taken up a position in the tree earlier," Sterling said with regret. "Now I'll have to do it the hard way."

"What are you going to do?" Lanna asked in alarm.

"I'll have to climb down the face of the bluff into the mimosa," Sterling replied, "though it would have been easier to simply climb the tree from the ground before the boars got here."

As the twins watched in fascinated silence, Sterling worked his way carefully down the face of the bluff, grasped the branches of the mimosa, and then swung himself into the tree. "He made it," Lanna exclaimed.

Carrying his homemade spear, the brave youth carefully advanced from branch to branch as he worked his way down the tree. Dathan spotted movement and turned to see two more wild boars saunter into the glen. Grunting and snorting, the newcomers tentatively approached the three boars already feeding, briefly touched noses, and then began to feed. All five of the wild boars seemed oblivious to Sterling's approach.

"Be careful, Sterling," Dathan called. "There are five instead of three."

Sterling had now reached the lowest branch and he carefully dropped to a prone position upon it. "Send Boris and Bortha," he requested.

Dathan gave the two boar hounds a gentle shove. "Go to Sterling," he ordered. Both dogs gave him a strange look.

"Boris, come here," Sterling called softly. "Bortha, come here."

At the sound of his voice both big dogs leaped to their feet, ran along the edge of the bluff with tails wagging, and whined as they looked down at Sterling as if trying to figure out how to get to him. "Come here," Sterling called again.

Boris turned and ran along the edge of the bluff. Reaching the slope that led down to the glen, he dashed down it with Bortha right on his heels. "Good dogs!" Sterling called. "Now bring the boars to me."

The big dogs seemed to know exactly what he wanted. Barking fiercely, they both charged at the five wild boars feeding under the oak. The wild pigs immediately forgot about the acorns. Wheeling about, they grouped together shoulder to shoulder and then charged straight at the two hounds, snarling and squealing in fury. Their screams of outrage filled the glen. Lanna cried out in fear. “They'll hurt the dogs!”

Boris and Bortha ran directly at the advancing line of wild pigs as if oblivious to the danger that they were facing. Dathan and Lanna held their breath, certain that both dogs would be slashed to pieces by the gleaming five-inch tusks. At the last possible moment, the brave boar hounds leaped to one side, circled behind the screaming boars, and slashed at their hind-quarters. The wild boars spun around, confused by the suddenness of the assault. Snarling and snapping, Boris and Bortha dashed among them, slashing at an exposed flank, biting at an ear, or crunching down on a foot and then leaping clear of the slashing tusks.

The wild boars were enraged. Screaming their hatred, they turned on the two dogs and slashed viciously with their sharp tusks in an attempt to disembowel the upstarts that were tormenting them so. But Boris and Bortha were like phantoms, leaping in and out with such speed that the confused pigs were never really sure where they were or from which direction the next attack would come.

“Bring them to me, Boris!” Sterling called. “Good work, Bortha! Bring them to me.”

Snarling and snapping and dancing about as if they enjoyed the fray, the dogs began to drive the five wild boars toward the tree. The wild pigs screamed their outrage, but they allowed themselves to be herded in the desired direction. Lanna began to cheer for the dogs. “Good girl, Bortha! Good boy, Boris! Look Dathan—they're doing it. They're taking the boars right where Sterling wants them!”

The five boars were now directly under the branch where Sterling waited. Snarling and snapping, the two hounds circled the furious boars, herding them together in a tight group. Sterling raised his spear.

And then, disaster struck. The twins heard a loud cracking, snapping sound and watched in horror as the branch broke, dropping Sterling into the middle of the screaming pigs. Sterling's cry of terror echoed across the glen.

Chapter Six

Lanna screamed. As the branch broke Sterling fell headfirst into the midst of the snarling wild boars. He rolled to his feet and leaped for the safety of the tree, but the furious animals were upon him in an instant, slashing and savaging him brutally. He disappeared beneath a mass of surging, twisting bodies. Lanna screamed again.

Boris and Bortha leaped into the fray like two warhorses charging into battle. Snarling with a ferocity that frightened even the twins, the two huge boar hounds slammed their bodies into the cluster of wild boars, knocking two or three of them over with the sheer force of the impact. Snarling, snapping, and growling furiously, the two hounds drove the boars away from the injured youth on the ground. Sterling crawled to the mimosa tree, pulled himself to a kneeling position, and attempted to climb up into the tree.

"Sterling, are you all right?" Dathan called.

"I'm hurt bad," Sterling replied.

One of the wild boars broke free from the group and charged toward the tree. Lanna screamed. "Sterling, look out!"

Roaring like a dragon, Boris charged at the boar and drove him back toward the group. Sterling sagged against the base of the tree. Dathan rose to his feet. "I have to help Sterling!"

Lanna grabbed his arm. "The boars will kill you!"

"They'll kill Sterling if they get to him again," Dathan replied gravely. His heart was in his throat as he dashed down the slope, keeping one eye on the grunting, squealing boars. So far, the dogs were keeping them away from the base of the mimosa. He ran to the tree, taking refuge momentarily behind the trunk. Boris and Bortha roared furiously as they continued to drive the wild boars away from Sterling.

Dathan darted around the mimosa and then stopped in horror as he saw the full extent of Sterling's injuries. The wild boars had managed to slash him several times, opening large gashes in his legs, side, and arm. Blood streamed from the wounds. Sterling's face was pale and drawn. "Help me," he said weakly.

Glancing once at the wild boars, Dathan seized Sterling's wrists and dragged him behind the trunk of the mimosa. Stooping down, he hefted his friend over his shoulder and then hurried back up the slope, stumbling a bit under the burden. When he reached Lanna he let Sterling's limp form slide to the ground. Lanna paled at the sight of the youth's injuries. "What shall we do for him, Dathan?"

"I—I really don't know what to do," Dathan stammered.

To the surprise of the twins, Sterling spoke. "My worst injury is to my right leg," he told them through trembling lips. "We have to stop the bleeding."

"W—What shall I do?" Dathan asked.

"Tear a piece from my doublet," Sterling whispered, grimacing against the pain that wracked his body. "Place it over the wound and press as firmly as you can to slow the bleeding." Dathan followed his directions.

A loud roar filled the air and the twins both glanced down toward the glen. Roaring like dragons intent on destroying all of Terrestria, the two big boar hounds charged furiously at the five wild boars, driving them from the glen. Squealing and grunting, the pigs ran from the clearing and disappeared into the undergrowth. Boris and Bortha stayed right behind them, snapping and slashing at their hind-quarters as they drove the wild beasts from the area.

Within moments, both dogs were back. They dashed up the slope and approached the three fugitives with tails wagging as if they were extremely pleased with themselves. "Well done, Boris and Bortha," Sterling said feebly.

"But for them, you would have been killed," Lanna told him soberly.

The injured youth nodded. "I know."

"I think the bleeding is slowing down," Dathan reported.

"Keep the pressure on," Sterling told him.

Dathan studied the injured youth for a long moment. Sterling's face was pale; his body trembled as if he were cold; and his numerous wounds were still bleeding, though the worst of the bleeding had slowed somewhat. Dathan could tell that Sterling was in terrible pain. "I need to go for help," Dathan told Lanna. "We need food, and Sterling's wounds need attention."

"We do need help," Sterling moaned through clenched teeth, "but we do not know whom we can trust. Karnivan sympathizers in this country are too numerous to count. We must be careful."

Dathan squeezed his shoulder as if to comfort him. "I will be careful," he promised, "but I must find someone who will help us."

Gritting his teeth against the waves of pain that coursed through his body, Sterling reached a trembling hand inside his doublet and withdrew a small compass and a parchment. "Use these."

Dathan unrolled the parchment and realized that he was looking at a homemade map of Northern Terrestria. Rivers, mountain ranges, villages, and towns were drawn in dark ink. "Head directly south," Sterling instructed him. "I think we're less than fifteen miles from the village of Wantrel." He gritted his teeth. "Perhaps there are villages that are closer where we can find help. Please hurry, but do be cautious."

Dathan nodded. "I'll do my best." He looked at Lanna. "Take care of him." He hurried down the slope, glancing at the compass to be certain that he was heading south.

What are we going to do for Sterling if I can't find help? he worried. *He's hurt bad, but I don't know what to do for him. What if he dies?* He took a deep breath. *And what are we going to do if we can't find food?*

Fifteen minutes later he spotted a thin column of smoke wafting upward above the trees and so he hurried toward it. He entered a small clearing to find a thin peasant leading a lively little donkey with a small cart loaded high with straw. Relief swept over Dathan. Perhaps help was at hand! He ran toward the man.

"Sir, can you help me?" he called.

The peasant turned at his salutation and Dathan saw a friendly, wrinkled face with lively eyes. "Certainly, lad. How may I help?" The man pulled on the donkey's halter to bring the animal to a halt.

"We're traveling—I'm traveling to a distant country and need your help, sir. I have a friend who is hurt bad—"

"The Judan boy?" the peasant asked.

Dathan felt a stab of fear. "H-how do y-you know about Sterling?" he stammered.

The old man laughed. "Is there a lass traveling with you?"

Dathan was alarmed at the old man's words. "How d-do you know about us?"

"Then you are the ones that the Karnivan soldiers are seeking."

Dathan was stunned. The man laid a hand on Dathan's arm. "Relax, son; you're among friends. We won't betray you to the Karnivans."

"But how do you know about us?"

"A company of Karnivan knights swept through here yesterday," the stranger replied. "They were looking for three young people, one of them a lass and one a Judan lad. I figure they are looking for you and your companions, aye?"

Dathan studied the man without answering. The man seemed friendly enough, but could he be trusted? "A whole company of Karnivans came here?" he asked finally.

"Well, not to my farm," the farmer replied. "Four soldiers came here asking questions and searching my farm, but others interrogated my neighbors and searched their farms. It seems that an entire company of Karnivan knights must have swept through the shire looking for you. What have you three done?"

Dathan decided to trust the man. "We haven't done anything wrong, sir, but our friend is Judan, and the Karnivans are searching for him. They'll either kill him or take him to Karniva and turn him over to Grimlor."

A thoughtful look crossed the man's face as he stroked the donkey's neck for a moment. "Lad, why would an entire company of knights search for one Judan lad? Who is he? What has he done?"

"I'm wondering the same thing, sir," Dathan answered truthfully. Without realizing what he was doing, he seized the man's tunic sleeve. "Can you help us, sir? Sterling is hurt bad, sir, and..."

"Hurt? What happened to him?"

"He was trying to hunt wild boars from a tree, sir, and the tree branch broke, dropping him among them. They cut him up pretty badly before the dogs drove them away."

"I see. How badly was he hurt?"

"He has several bad gashes on his legs and at least one on his side and one on his arm. He's cut up pretty badly."

The man winced. "Where is he now?"

"Maybe a mile due north of here."

"Hm-m. Pretty rough terrain. We'd never get the cart through. Let me unhitch the cart and then Ebenezer and I will see if we can't bring your friend here."

Relief swept over Dathan. "Thank you, sir."

"Aye." The farmer quickly unhitched the donkey from the cart. "Well, lad, let me tell my wife what we're doing and then we'll be on our way." He hurried toward the humble little cottage and then returned in less than a minute with a leather satchel. "Lead the way, son."

Dathan checked the compass and then started due north with the farmer and the donkey right behind him. "My name is Melzar," the farmer told him.

"I am honored, sir. And I am Dathan."

The sun was dropping behind the ridges to the west as they approached the glen where the accident had taken place. Leaving the donkey waiting patiently in the glen, Dathan and Melzar hurried up the slope to the knoll where Lanna and Sterling waited. The dogs bounded forward to greet them.

"How is he?" Dathan asked his sister.

Lanna sighed. "I don't know. He's been asleep, or maybe unconscious, ever since you left."

Melzar knelt beside the injured youth, took one quick look at his injuries, and then pulled a knife, small rolls of cloth, and a vial from his satchel. Working swiftly, he exposed Sterling's injuries, poured in some sort of ointment, and then bound up the wounds. "Will—will he live?" Lanna asked with tear-filled eyes.

"He's lost a lot of blood," Melzar told her gently, "but he's young and he's strong. I think he'll make it."

Lanna nodded gratefully.

"Well, lad, we need to get your friend to the house as quickly as possible. Help me carry him down to Ebenezer, will you?"

The darkness of night swept over the little farm as the little donkey stopped with his heavy burden right beside the door of the humble cottage. A rectangle of yellow light splashed across the yard as the door opened to reveal the smiling face of a thin woman. In one hand she carried a flickering lamp. "Welcome," she greeted the weary travelers. "Bring your friend into the house so that we may care for him. You are welcome here."

A feeling of peace swept over Dathan as he and Melzar carried the still form of Sterling into the little cottage. As they laid him on a narrow frame bed, Sterling opened his eyes. He studied their worried faces for a moment and then looked around the room. "Where am I?" he asked.

"You are among friends, Sterling," the farmer answered.

Sterling's eyes widened at the use of his name and he looked questioningly at Dathan. "I think you're in good hands," Dathan told him. "Melzar bound up your wounds and helped me bring you here."

The woman stepped to the fireplace where a cheerful fire danced on the hearth. Lifting a dipper from a small kettle at the fire's edge, she poured a dark liquid into an earthenware cup. "My name is Miriam," she told her visitors as she approached the bed. "I am Melzar's wife." She handed the cup to Sterling. "Drink this," she instructed. "It will give you strength."

Sterling sat up, drank the contents of the cup, and then lay back down. Within moments, he was sound asleep.

"Sit and rest," Melzar told Lanna and Dathan. "I will tend to Ebenezer and your dogs while Miriam gets supper." Taking the lamp, he headed out into the darkness of the night. Dathan glanced at Sterling and then hurried to follow Melzar.

Spotting the yellow glow of the lantern, Dathan made his way through the darkness and found the old farmer drawing a bucket of water from a well. "We'll feed your dogs right after supper," the man told Dathan, "but I figure they could use a good drink right now." Boris and Bortha waited at his feet as if they knew that the water was intended for them.

After giving the water to the dogs, Dathan helped Melzar hitch Ebenezer to the cart and take the load of hay to a small barn. "Fork a bit of hay into Ebenezer's manger while I give him a rub down," the old man requested. He patted the donkey's neck. "You've put in a long day, haven't you, old friend?"

Dathan found a three-tined pitchfork and set to work to fill the narrow manger while Melzar lovingly tended to the little donkey. "So you're helping your Judan friend escape the Karnivans, are you, son?" the old man said with a chuckle. "Just how far do you intend to run?"

"We intend to go all the way to Eastern Ainranon," Dathan replied.

The old man glanced at him in surprise. "Eastern Ainranon! Lad, do you know how far that is?"

Dathan nodded. "We figure we have to cross the southern half of Cheswold, all of Karniva, and most of Ainranon. I know we're in for quite a trek."

"Do you realize how many Karnivan knights are searching for you?"

"I don't suppose there is any way to know, sir."

Melzar began to curry the donkey's coat. "The shire was overrun with them yesterday."

Dathan looked at the old farmer in surprise. "Overrun, sir? How many do you mean by that? Are you talking about a whole company of knights?"

"More than that, lad. Perhaps hundreds."

"Hundreds?" Dathan was stunned. "Why would hundreds of Karnivans be searching for us?"

The old man studied his face. "I thought perhaps you could tell me. Who are you? What have you done?"

The youth shook his head. "We haven't done anything, sir. My sister and I are trying to help Sterling escape to Ainranon to elude the Karns; that's all."

"So what do you know about Sterling? What has he done? Why are the Karnivans pursuing him?"

Dathan frowned at the old man's questions. "I really don't know, sir. Three days ago my sister and I saw a company of Karnivan knights capture Sterling right outside our castle. Knowing that he would be killed if he were sent to Grimlor, I helped him escape the dungeon and we decided to help him in his flight to Ainranon. We've only known him for three days, sir."

Melzar was thoughtful. "I see. But you have no idea who he is or where he is from?"

"Nay, sir. His regal clothing would cause one to think that perhaps he is royalty, or at the least, nobility."

The old man nodded at this. "So it would seem. But perhaps you should find out more about him, lad."

"There hasn't been much time for talk, sir. We've been running for our lives."

Melzar smiled. "Aye, that makes sense." He was silent for a moment. "Perhaps it is time for a long talk with your friend Sterling. Perhaps it is time for you to ask him just who he is and why it seems that the entire Karnivan army is pursuing him."

Dathan set the tines of the wooden pitchfork against the floor. "Sterling is Judan, sir. The Karns have sworn to kill every last Judan in Terrestria."

Melzar shook his head. "There's more to it than that. Grimlor and the Karnivans are attempting to take over Cheswold. Do you think they would send this many knights to capture just one Judan youth? Nay, lad. Your friend Sterling must be of great importance to them, or they would not pursue him so relentlessly."

Dathan nodded. "I have been wondering about it."

The old man turned toward the house. "Well, we'll have some time to think about it. You and your friend aren't going anywhere until his wounds heal. That will be a week or two at the very least." He smiled at Dathan. "We want you to stay here, of course. Come on, let's go see if Miriam has supper ready, shall we?"

"We appreciate your generosity, sir."

"This farm is the ideal hideaway, lad," Melzar replied with a thoughtful look in his eyes. "If you have to lay low while the Karnivans search for you, there's no better place to do it than right here. The farm is a bit secluded and almost no one ever comes out here. Still, we can't be too careful. There are a few Karnivan sympathizers in the shire and any one of them would turn you in to the soldiers. I can think of one man in particular who would like nothing better. His name is Akbar. If he ever learned that you were here, your lives would be in great danger."

Chapter Seven

The next few days passed swiftly for Lanna and Dathan. Melzar proved to be an excellent host and did everything in his power to let the three unexpected guests know that they were welcome on his farm and safe in his care. Cheerful and friendly, he seemed determined to be an encouragement to the three young travelers, and they soon came to trust him.

Dathan in particular enjoyed the company of the vigorous old man. It had been months since the youth had seen his own father, and the abusive treatment he and Lanna had received at the hands of Garven and other servants at Windstone Castle had nearly extinguished any spark of hope for a better future. He reveled in the kindness shown to him by the gentle farmer. Melzar's presence in his life was temporary at best, yet it met a desperate need in his lonely heart.

Gracious and thoughtful, Melzar's wife Miriam had met the same needs for Lanna. The twins' mother had died giving birth to Lanna and Dathan, and therefore Lanna had never known the sweetness of a mother's love. She found it in the gentle hands and kind words of the farmer's wife.

Sterling's wounds healed slowly, and Dathan could tell that his energetic friend found his confinement to the tiny farmhouse almost unbearable. His injuries were not life-threatening, but they were extremely painful and kept him from helping Melzar and Dathan with the farm work. All three young people were anxious to be on the road again, but Sterling especially chafed at the delay.

"Lad, did your father ever teach you the use of the sword?" Melzar asked one day as he and Dathan were putting up hay. Dathan turned, taken by surprise at the abruptness of the question, and was stunned to see a gleaming sword in the old farmer's hands.

The boy took a quick step backward. "Nay, sir, I have never even touched a sword. My father is a craftsman, not a knight."

"Skill with the sword is not for the knight alone," the old farmer countered. He chuckled and extended the hilt of the weapon toward Dathan. "Here. Don't be afraid of it, lad. Take it."

Dathan took a deep breath and reached for the sword. As his fingers touched the hilt it seemed that a jolt of power leaped from the weapon and shot through his hands. He leaped back in alarm. "Don't be afraid of it, lad," Melzar encouraged. "It won't hurt you. The only person who has to fear this sword is the man on whom you draw it."

The boy's hands trembled as he took the gleaming weapon. Holding it with both hands, he turned the sword slowly, admiring the polished steel of the blade, the detailed engravings of knights and dragons in the guard, and the feeling of power that the weight of the weapon gave. He let out his breath in a long, slow sigh, and for just an instant, he could almost imagine himself swinging the magnificent weapon in battle. In the center of the handle was a crest emblazoned with a cross and a crown. His heart leaped. King Emmanuel's coat of arms!

"You have an enemy, lad...actually, many of them. I think it would be good for you to learn to handle the sword."

Dathan looked at him in alarm. "Me, sir? But I am not a knight."

"The use of the sword is not for the knight alone," the old farmer repeated. "I am no knight, yet I have trained for years with the sword. It is best to be prepared to fight when the need arises."

Dathan studied the wrinkled face, marveling at the intense look that suddenly appeared in the old man's eyes. "Have you ever had to fight, sir? With a sword, I mean."

Melzar looked away quickly. "Aye, there have been times, lad."

Dathan sensed that the question somehow brought back painful memories and so he changed the subject. "Are you serious in saying that I should learn to handle a sword, sir?"

"Aye."

Dathan took an experimental swing with the weapon, enjoying the sensation of power that he suddenly felt. The tip of the blade passed within a foot of Melzar's tunic and the farmer leaped back in alarm. "Careful, lad! Take it easy with that until you know what you are doing."

The boy lowered the sword, suddenly feeling very foolish and awkward. "I'm sorry, sir." He hung his head. "I didn't mean to—"

The farmer's gentle laugh interrupted him. "Don't take it to heart, lad. There's no harm done." He pulled his tunic away from his chest and looked down at it as if to inspect the fabric for damage. He grinned suddenly and Dathan realized that the inspection of the tunic was the old man's way of teasing him. "To tell the truth, I did the very same thing the first time I got my hands on a sword."

Dathan was relieved. "Honest?"

Melzar nodded. "I suppose it's the natural thing to do, lad. What good is a sword if you can't swing it? And if you're going to swing it, you might as well swing it with all your might, aye?" He gave Dathan a sheepish look. "Actually, now that I think of it, I did a bit of damage that day."

Dathan's curiosity was aroused. "Damage? What did you do?"

The old man chuckled at the memory. "I took a mighty swing with the sword, and I accidentally cut down a sapling cherry tree that my father had planted for my mother. She was furious when she learned what I had done. As I remember, my father saved my life that day by talking my mother out of using the sword on me." He and Dathan laughed together.

The boy slowly turned the sword as he again admired the weapon's great beauty. "This sword is magnificent, sir! Where did you get it?"

A faraway look came into the old farmer's eyes and he turned and stared out across the field.

Dathan raised his voice. "Sir, where—"

"I heard you the first time, lad. The sword was given to me by my father on the day that he died. It had been given to him by his father. Actually, it has been in our family for many generations."

Dathan held the gleaming weapon with an awe that bordered on reverence. "It's magnificent, sir, the finest sword I've ever seen. It will be an honor to learn to fight with it."

The old man laughed as he took the sword from Dathan. "Actually, lad, you will start your training with a mock sword made of wood. You won't handle this one again until you have an idea of what you are going to do with it."

Slightly embarrassed, Dathan nodded. "I understand, sir. When will I start training?"

Melzar put a thin hand on his shoulder. "Well, there's no time like the present. We can finish the haying this afternoon—suppose we start your training right this minute?"

"I'd like that, sir."

"Wait right here." Melzar hurried into the barn and returned in a moment without the magnificent sword. Instead he carried two simple wooden swords, one of which he handed to Dathan. "We'll start with defense," he told the anxious youth. "First and foremost, the sword is used to defend oneself against an attack. Learning to defend oneself is more important than learning to press an attack."

Dathan hefted the mock sword and made a couple of short cuts with it, disappointed that it lacked the feel of the real sword. Melzar read the disappointment in his eyes. "We'll get to the real sword soon enough, lad," he reassured him. "But this way you can learn the basics of swordplay without hurting yourself."

He stepped a few paces away from Dathan. "Let me show you the importance of the sword's use in defense. Come at me with your sword."

"Sir?"

"Come at me," the farmer repeated. "Attack me with your sword."

Dathan studied the old man, noting the stooped posture, the thin, feeble limbs, and the slight tremor in the hands. "Are you sure, sir? I don't want to hurt you."

Melzar laughed. "Give me your best attack, lad. You won't hurt me."

The boy hesitated.

"Come on, lad, I want to see your best. Attack me as if you need to kill me to defend your family."

Dathan let out his breath in a long sigh. "Are you sure, sir?"

"Your most ferocious attack, lad. Don't hold anything back."

Screaming with all his might, the youth rushed the old farmer. As he neared Melzar's position, he raised the sword and brought it down in a ferocious forward slice. To his astonishment, Melzar calmly met the wooden blade with the flat of his own blade, easily deflecting the blow. Without giving the old man a moment to recover, Dathan raised his sword over his left shoulder and brought it across Melzar's chest in a vicious backhanded cut. Just as before, the attack was deflected by the farmer's sword. Twisting to the right to gain added momentum, Dathan drew the wooden weapon far back and then brought it across in an incredibly fast horizontal cut. To his amazement, Melzar's sword flashed upward, deflecting the force of the blow and sending Dathan's sword skyward in a lazy, tumbling arc that terminated with the weapon landing five paces behind him.

Dathan turned and stared at the sword and then looked back at his opponent. "How—how did you do that?"

"It's a defensive technique I'll teach you later," the old man replied.

"That's amazing! That's the most amazing thing I have ever seen!"

Melzar grinned. "Do you see the importance of a good defense, lad?"

Dathan nodded eagerly as he turned to retrieve his sword. "Aye, sir, that I do."

"The key to a good defense," his mentor told him, "is knowing what your opponent is going to do before he does it."

"That's impossible, sir," the boy replied, picking up his sword and stepping toward the old man. "I can't read people's minds."

"Nay, but you can learn to anticipate an opponent's moves before he makes them."

Dathan was puzzled. "How?"

"Just now you made three attempts to strike me with your sword, yet each time you told me what you were going to do before you did it."

Now Dathan was really puzzled. "How did I do that, sir?"

"You told me with your body."

"My body? What do you mean?"

"For example, when you prepared to make your third swing, you twisted your right shoulder back, shifted your weight to your right leg, and lifted your left foot slightly. The angle of your wrist told me that you intended to attempt a horizontal cut. Your eyes told me the exact moment when the move would come. Son, your entire body was sending signals!"

Dathan grinned sheepishly. "That obvious, huh?"

"As you gain experience, you'll learn to watch your opponent's eyes, his footwork, the attitude of his shoulders, even the set of his jaw. I'll teach you to anticipate every move he's going to make before he makes it. By studying your opponent, you'll know his fighting style better than he does. You'll know his strengths and his weaknesses. You'll be prepared to counter every move he makes."

The boy sighed. "I didn't know that sword fighting was going to be this complicated. How will I ever learn all this?"

"There's more to swordplay than just swinging a sword," Melzar agreed. "Anyone can swing a sword and chop down a cherry tree. But an experienced swordsman wields his sword with a power that comes from knowledge—he studies his opponent until he knows the enemy's strengths and weaknesses and can anticipate exactly how he is going to attack."

"But what happens when you go against an enemy that you have never met?" Dathan argued. "You know, like in a battle?"

"The first few seconds are the most critical," the old man replied. "In those few seconds you must learn these things about your enemy. Once you know how to defend yourself against his methods, you will also know how to press the attack and defeat him."

The youth shook his head. "I never knew there was this much to it."

"You won't learn it in a day," the old farmer told him with a smile. "Now, get a good grip on your sword and come at me again. Do it in slow motion, for I want you to watch me closely and see what I do to fend off your moves. I'll explain as we go along. Ready? All right, press the attack!"

Dathan took a deep breath and then charged across the barnyard with his sword raised.

Dathan and Melzar trained every day with the swords. Dathan was an apt pupil; his mentor was a master; and the youth's skills developed quickly. After three days the wooden swords were abandoned for real ones. "You've learned quickly," Melzar told Dathan, as he parried a thrust and then countered with a horizontal slice of his own, which Dathan deflected. "You're confident, yet not overconfident, and that's good. Your reflexes are a bit slow perhaps and your footwork a bit clumsy, but I've never seen anyone fight with as much enthusiasm as you. You're putting your whole heart into this, and that more than compensates for your lack of experience and skill. You have the heart of a lion. It won't be long before you'll be ready for a real battle."

"I've had an outstanding teacher," Dathan replied. "It's obvious that you know how to handle a sword." He feinted with his shoulders as though to wield the sword in a horizontal cut and then abruptly swung the weapon in a surprise uppercut in an attempt to catch the old master off guard.

"Aye, I know the proper use of the sword," the old farmer replied modestly as he easily met Dathan's blow and deflected it, "but you have an intensity that is seldom found in one so young. If you continue to apply yourself with all your heart, lad, there's no reason you could not quickly become a master swordsman, able to hold your own against any knight in Terrestria."

"So this is what you've been doing," a voice called, and both combatants turned to see Sterling approaching. "This whole time I've been suffering in the house, I thought you two were working, but now I find that you've been playing knights instead."

"Dathan is learning an art that may one day save his life," the old farmer said shortly, and Dathan glanced at him in surprise, for the farmer's tone was gruff. "As it happens, he's actually quite good for a beginner. He'll be a master before long."

"I could take him," Sterling said boldly. "Just give me a stave."

"Aye, could you now?" Melzar replied. His irritation was evident in his face.

Sterling shrugged. "I could if I had a stave. There's not a sword in Terrestria fast enough to beat a good man with a stave."

"Well, you'll get your chance to make good on your words," the old man retorted, "for I just happen to have a pike pole that will serve as the stave you are looking for. Wait right here." He hurried to the barn and returned within moments with a long pike, which he handed to Sterling. "Six-and-a-half feet, to be exact," he told the youth. "Now, let's see what you can do with it."

He handed Dathan one of the mock swords and took the real one. "I want you to use wood," he told Dathan, reading the disappointment in his eyes. "I won't have you hurting each other."

"Let him use steel," Sterling said diffidently. "I'm not afraid of him."

Melzar turned and gazed at him for several long moments without speaking. "I said he'll use wood."

Sterling nodded.

"Gentlemen, let's see what you are made of. Three blows to the limbs or one blow to the torso wins this little tournament. You don't have helmets, so avoid giving blows to the face or head. Ready? Go at it!"

With these words, Melzar quickly stepped from between the challengers and the skirmish began. Dathan advanced slowly toward Sterling, watching him carefully as Melzar had taught him and waiting for Sterling to make the first move. Holding the pike at waist level, Sterling circled warily, feinting two or three times with the pike to throw Dathan off guard. Sword ready, Dathan waited.

Sterling took half a step backward and then suddenly leaped directly at Dathan, thrusting the end of the pike at his chest. Dathan sidestepped and parried the thrust with his sword, but before he had time to recover he found himself knocked off his feet. Sterling had swung the other end of the pike from behind and swept his feet out from under him! As Dathan landed on his back his opponent leaped forward and pinned his chest to the ground with the end of the pike. "Yield!" he cried, "for I have you!"

Dathan let out his breath in a long sigh. "I yield."

Sterling grinned at him as he let him up. "Give me a stave over a sword any day," he exulted. He turned and looked at Melzar for approval.

"You've had some experience with a stave," the farmer observed as he hurried forward. "I could tell that this was not your first time." Sterling grinned. "But you're overconfident and you moved in without taking the time to study your opponent," Melzar continued. "Lad, that's not wise."

The youth shrugged. "I took Dathan out."

"Only because he is a beginner," Melzar shot back. "He has the makings of a good swordsman, but he lacks experience. Had you gone up against an experienced swordsman, the outcome would have been quite different."

Sterling shrugged again. "I'd go against an experienced swordsman."

"Would you, now?"

"Aye."

"Then prepare your stave, for I am your next challenger."

Sterling was visibly surprised by the challenge. "You, sir?" He seemed a bit amused as he looked the farmer over, and Dathan knew exactly what he was thinking: Melzar was simply too old and decrepit to offer much of a match.

"Aye, lad."

"Very well, sir." Sterling raised the stave.

Holding the sword at waist level, the old farmer circled the youth. With a troubled look on his face, Sterling watched the old man warily, and Dathan realized that he was beginning to have second thoughts about the skirmish. Each combatant studied the other closely, guardedly, waiting for a sudden move.

Melzar took two quick steps toward Sterling, raising his sword abruptly. Sterling took half a step forward as he did, raising the pike at a diagonal to fend off the blow. The old man stepped back without following through with an attack.

Sterling leaped forward at that instant, swinging the pike barely ten inches above the ground with a two-handed move that was intended to knock Melzar's legs from beneath him. To the astonishment of both boys, the old man nimbly leaped over the swinging stave, tapped Sterling hard on the upper arm with the flat of his sword, and then leaped clear. "That's one," he called briskly. "In a real battle, lad, you would have just lost an arm."

Dathan saw a look of anger and frustration cross Sterling's face, but then it disappeared as quickly as it had come. The youth feinted with the stave two or three times and then abruptly rushed at Melzar with the weapon held at waist level. The old man rolled under the stave as it passed, striking Sterling in the back of the thigh once again with the flat of his sword. "That's two, lad."

The youth spun around, taking a deep breath and letting it back out to vent his frustration. Warily, he stepped in close and began a series of vigorous blows and thrusts with the pike. Melzar met each one with the edge of his sword, leaving a deep gash in the wood each time. Sterling continued the frenzied volley of blows and thrusts relentlessly for more than a minute without letting up or pausing to catch his breath. Melzar stood his ground under the relentless onslaught, effortlessly meeting each blow with his sword and refusing to give an inch of ground, although the tall youth pressed him hard. Finally, winded and nearly exhausted, Sterling backed away and lowered his stave for a moment's rest.

It was at that instant that Melzar struck, moving with the speed and agility of a panther. Leaping directly at the surprised youth, he unleashed a volley of cuts and combinations that Sterling struggled to counter with the pike. Within moments he was retreating, driven backwards by the ferocity of the old man's attack. Dathan was amazed at the speed of the farmer's sword.

Sterling wearily countered a series of lightning-quick cuts and slices, and then tried a thrust of his own with the stave.

Melzar merely sidestepped and then caught the pole with his free hand, twisting it hard as he thrust abruptly upward. The resulting force against the pike pole threw Sterling off balance, and the old man was ready. He threw his shoulder against the youth's chest, sending him to the ground and wrenching the stave from his grasp.

The youth hit the ground hard and lay still for a moment or two. The stunned look on his face showed he couldn't quite believe it had really happened. At last, he got to his feet slowly.

"King Emmanuel has chosen the sword as our weapon of defense," Melzar said quietly. "Aye, you're fast, lad, and it's obvious that you have trained well with the stave. Your footwork and your movements with the stave tell me that you've had quite a bit of experience. But I would encourage you to train with the sword, for it is the weapon that our King has chosen for us."

Sterling shrugged. "I still prefer the stave."

"Sterling, you're bleeding!" Dathan called as he saw a large red stain seeping through the fabric of Sterling's doublet. "You're hurt!"

"I've opened up the wound in my side again," Sterling observed.

"Lad, I'm sorry," Melzar said quietly as he rushed forward. "I forgot about your injuries. I never should have allowed you to compete."

"I'll be all right, though I suppose I should head for the house and get this bandaged," the tall youth replied. Holding the heel of his hand against his side to staunch the bleeding, he hurried toward the farmhouse.

Dathan looked at Melzar with awe. "You were amazing!"

The old farmer shook his head. "My sword came from King Emmanuel himself," he replied quietly, "and its strength is merely a reflection of his majesty and power." He looked into Dathan's eyes and Dathan saw a tenderness in his gaze that he had never noticed. "Miriam and I have no children of our own," the man said quietly. "The King's sword has been in our family for generations, and yet..."

Here he paused and looked toward the house as if he had just remembered that Sterling's wound needed attention. "Lad, we can talk of this later." Leaving Dathan staring wordlessly after him, he hurried toward the house, still carrying the magnificent sword.

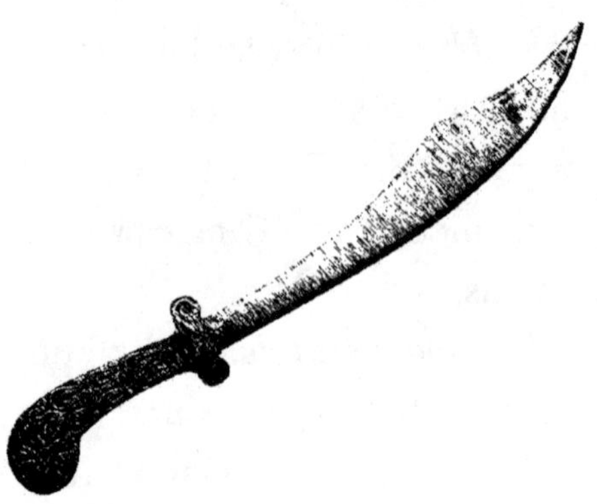

Chapter Eight

Melzar and Dathan trained with the swords every day after that. The wound in Sterling's side seemed reluctant to heal and gave him trouble for more than a week, so he never again participated in the skirmishes. Dathan applied himself during the exercises, watching Melzar's every move with the sword, studying his footwork, noting how and when he chose to advance and when he decided to retreat. He recognized that the old farmer, in spite of his age and physical condition, was still a master swordsman. The youth wisely set out to learn everything that he could from him.

Dathan wondered for days about the magnificent sword. Could it be true that it had come from King Emmanuel himself? What a privilege it would be to own such a sword! The weapon was magnificent to look at, to be sure, with its ornate golden handle and gleaming steel blade, but its real value lay in the fact that it had come from the King. Dathan sensed that the splendid weapon possessed an unusual power that other swords did not. More than once Melzar had stressed that the sword would never harm anyone who was loyal to the King; yet could easily defeat and destroy one who was not.

One afternoon Dathan sat in the shade of the elm beside

the barn, waiting for Melzar and watching Lanna help Miriam with the washing. Sterling sat on a stool just outside the door of the house, peeling potatoes to help Miriam with supper. *I wonder what Melzar was going to tell me that day just after he and Sterling fought,* Dathan thought. *For a moment, I thought he was going to tell me that he was going to give me the sword!* He sighed. *What a magnificent weapon!*

"I want you to go into town with me," Melzar's voice announced, jarring Dathan from his reverie. "The blacksmith has made a new wheel for the cart and I need to pick it up. I thought you might enjoy seeing our little village."

"Would it be safe?" Dathan asked. "We *are* trying to keep out of sight of the Karns, you know."

"Aye, it wouldn't be safe to take all three of you," the farmer replied. "Someone might put two and two together and realize that you three are the ones the Karnivans are looking for. But if it's just you, I think everything will be fine. If anyone should ask any questions, just say that you are a friend of mine. That should satisfy anyone's curiosity."

Within moments the little donkey was hitched to the cart and off to town they went with Melzar sitting on the seat and Dathan riding in the back. The day was sunny, but a cold wind swept down from the fells. "Well, your friend's wounds are healing quite nicely," the farmer observed, as the cart bounced along the narrow road. "Within three or four days you should be able to resume your journey."

"I know we need to travel to Ainranon as soon as possible," Dathan replied wistfully, "but I hate to think of leaving you and Miriam. You've been like grandparents to us, and we sure have enjoyed staying here."

"Aye, lad," came the quiet reply, "and we will surely miss you when you leave."

"Thank you for teaching me how to use the sword," Dathan told the old man. "I know that I still have a lot to learn, but you have taught me well, and for that I am grateful. Some day I will have a sword of my own."

"It has been a pleasure to teach you," Melzar said. "Seldom does one find a pupil so eager to learn. And as I told you before, you have the heart of a lion. Your reflexes are keen and your timing is improving. Lad, if you continue to apply yourself you will one day be a master swordsman."

"Sir, let me ask you something..." For the rest of the journey, the man and the boy talked of nothing but the use of the sword, with Dathan asking numerous questions and the old master patiently answering each one.

"Well, lad, this is our little village," Melzar said as the cart approached a small cluster of shops and daub-and-wattle houses nestled in the pine-shrouded foothills of a forbidding mountain range.

"By what name is the village called, sir?"

Melzar laughed. "The village is too small to have a proper name, lad. Folks simply call it 'the village.' " Unguided by the slack reins in his master's hands, Ebenezer skillfully maneuvered the cart down the narrow street that bisected the village, carefully guiding the cart around potholes, sleeping dogs, and children at play.

"Please, sire, have mercy!" a young voice cried in fear. "I won't do it again! Please, sire!"

Dathan looked down the street to see a small crowd gathering. He turned to Melzar. "What's happening?"

"Let's go see," the farmer replied, halting Ebenezer with a gentle tug on the reins and then hopping nimbly from the cart. Dathan scrambled down to join him. Together, they approached the small crowd.

In the center of the ring of townspeople, a tall, bearded man with cruel eyes and an angry countenance had a firm grip on the tattered tunic of a struggling boy. In the other hand the man held a large knife. Terror was written across the face of the desperate boy and his eyes were filled with tears. "Please, sire," he begged again. "I'll never do it again! Show mercy, I beg you!"

"Why should I show mercy?" The man's words came out as an angry snarl. "You know the penalty for stealing."

Melzar pushed through the ring of spectators. "What's going on, Akbar?"

The tall man glanced at Melzar, and Dathan saw that his eyes were filled with contempt. "This is none of your affair, old man."

"Oh, but it is," Melzar said quietly but forcefully. "Was the boy stealing from you?"

"Aye," Akbar growled. "He stole an apple from my fruit stand."

"And what do you intend to do about it, Akbar?"

The tall merchant's face was filled with hatred as he brandished the knife. "This little thief is going to lose a finger!" Releasing his grip on the boy's threadbare tunic, Akbar seized the boy's thin wrist and lifted it forcefully. The youth screamed with fear.

Melzar addressed the terrified boy. "Lad, did you steal from this man?"

The boy lifted his eyes and looked directly at Melzar. "Aye, sire, I did."

"Why, lad?"

"I'm not excusing myself, sire, but I'm hungry. Mama and I haven't eaten in two days."

Melzar took a deep breath and let it out slowly. He turned to Akbar. "And you intend to cut off a finger for the theft of one apple."

The angry man shrugged. "It's the custom, Melzar; you know that. And I daresay that this little thief will think twice before he ever steals from me again." Akbar scanned the crowd to read their reactions, but the townspeople were silent and uncommitted.

Melzar turned to the trembling boy. "What do you have to say for yourself, lad? Can you think of any good reason why you shouldn't lose a finger for your theft?"

Tears flowed down the dirty face. "Nay, sire." The boy turned to face Akbar. "I'm sorry, sire, for stealing from you. I won't do it again."

"I'll say you won't," Akbar raged. He lifted the knife, intending to carry out his threat.

"Wait a moment," Melzar interrupted. "There is no need to go through with this; the boy is repentant. And I will pay you for the apple."

"Stay out of this, Melzar," the merchant growled. "You can't stop me from serving justice on a thief."

"I will pay you for five apples," the old farmer offered. "Let the boy go, Akbar. I appeal to you to show mercy."

Akbar said nothing, but his eyes glittered with fury. It was obvious that he fully intended to carry out his threat and he resented Melzar for standing in his way. "If you choose to harm this boy in front of all these people," Melzar argued, "your business will wither and die like a flower dropped on the hot pavement."

"Stay out of this, old man," Akbar growled through clenched teeth. "You can't stop me from serving justice on this wretched little thief." Trembling with rage, the merchant dragged the terrified boy against the wall of his shop. He raised the knife.

It happened too quickly for the eye to follow. Melzar leaped forward, seized Akbar's wrist, and slammed the knuckles of his knife hand against the door post. The weapon dropped from Akbar's hand and Melzar caught it before it hit the ground. The angry merchant stared at the old farmer, too stunned to react. A startled gasp went up from the crowd of spectators.

Dathan fully expected Akbar to explode in fury. To his amazement, the man released his hold on the boy and began rubbing the knuckles of his injured hand. "Pay me for the apples," he demanded, "and then get this filthy wretch out of my sight."

The knife had somehow disappeared and Melzar was already handing Akbar two copper coins. The farmer put his hand on the shoulder of the sobbing boy. "Run along now, lad, and don't steal any more apples."

"Nay, sire, I won't, sire. I thank you, sire." Without another word, the boy disappeared down the street.

Akbar leaned down until his face was mere inches from Melzar's. "I'll settle this with you later," he threatened in a low voice, "out at your farm where there will be no witnesses. You'll pay for this, old man." Dathan saw the hatred glittering in the man's eyes and had no doubt that he meant every word.

Akbar's angry gaze fell upon Dathan. "Who are you?" he demanded. "I haven't seen you around before."

In that instant, Dathan remembered Melzar's words. "I can think of one man in particular who would like nothing better than to turn you in to the soldiers. His name is Akbar. If he ever learned that you were here, your lives would be in great danger." *Akbar!* Dathan thought in desperation. *This is the very man that Melzar warned us about!*

"Who are you, boy?" Akbar demanded again.

"I—I'm just a friend of Melzar," Dathan replied nervously, and his voice cracked as he spoke.

"A friend, eh? Where are you from?"

Dathan looked around in desperation. The crowd was dispersing as the villagers drifted away. Akbar seized the front of his tunic in an iron grip. "Where are you from, boy?"

Melzar stepped forward. "Leave the lad alone, Akbar. As he told you, he is a friend of mine."

The big man released his hold on Dathan. He took a step back, but his eyes narrowed as he thought the matter through. His face tightened and a look of recognition swept across his angry features. He pointed a dirty finger at the frightened youth. "I know who you are—you're one of the three runaways! The ones the Karnivan knights were searching for!"

Dathan's heart constricted with fear.

"Don't be absurd, Akbar," Melzar challenged. "That was a week ago."

Akbar's face registered his confusion as he considered Melzar's words. Shaking his head, he turned and entered his shop. "Do you think he knows?" Dathan whispered to Melzar.

"I don't know," the old man said thoughtfully, and his eyes betrayed the fact that he was worried. "We need to get that wheel and get back home as soon as possible. If Akbar gives this any more thought, we could be facing serious trouble."

Later that evening, Miriam lifted a steaming kettle of rabbit stew from the hearth and carried it to the table. "This will be the richest stew I have ever served," she observed happily. "How did you bag so many rabbits, Melzar?"

"Actually, I didn't," her husband replied. "Sterling caught them all in those snares he set up at the edge of the forest."

"The lad must know what he's doing," the woman declared. "I've never seen so many." She took her seat at the table and

Melzar sent a petition of thanksgiving to King Emmanuel. "The stew is still very hot," Miriam told her guests. "Why don't you pass me your bowls?"

A loud knock at the door startled everyone. The door burst open before Melzar could even rise from his seat and a breathless young boy rushed into the room. "Aunt Miriam, come quickly!" he cried. "Papa sent me! Mama's about to give birth!"

Miriam immediately rose to her feet but Melzar put a hand on her arm. "Eat first, my love. The baby will wait another moment or two."

She stared at him. "I couldn't eat a bite if I tried, knowing that Martha and the baby need me."

Her husband shrugged. "I knew you would say that. Do you want me to take you?"

Miriam shook her head. "Just hitch up Ebenezer and I'll take the cart." She turned to the boy. "Mark, how did you get here?"

"I ran, Aunt Miriam."

"The whole three miles?"

"Aye, Aunt Miriam."

Melzar was on his way out the door when he spun around and addressed his three guests. "Just start eating without us," he suggested. "I'll be back in a few minutes, but Miriam will be a bit longer."

Lanna looked up at Miriam. "How long will you be gone, ma'am?"

The farmer's wife laughed. "That all depends on the baby, dear." She bustled about the cottage, gathering the necessary items to assist with the baby's arrival.

Melzar came back in just as she was finishing her preparations. "Hurry, dear," he told her. "It will be dark in another quarter hour. Do you want me to light a lamp?"

"I'll be fine without it," she told him. She gave him a kiss, and she and Mark went out the door.

"Is Mark your nephew?" Lanna asked.

"Well, actually, he's our great nephew," Melzar replied. "His father is Miriam's nephew." He glanced at the table. "You three haven't started," he observed. "The stew's going to get cold."

"We were waiting for you, sir," Sterling told him.

"Well, let's get started, shall we?" the old man said with a grin. "If it's as good as it smells, it won't last long."

They were just finishing the meal when Boris and Bortha began barking furiously. Sterling stood and hurried to the door. "I wonder what has the dogs so upset."

"Probably just a raccoon or a skunk or something," Melzar said with a laugh.

Sterling opened the door and took one look. An expression of panic swept across his face. "Sir, we're in trouble!"

Melzar ran to the door and the twins were right behind him. The night was dark, with not a single star in the sky. Twenty flickering points of light were bobbing up and down in the darkness of the night as they swept up the narrow lane that led to Melzar's little farm. "A score of mounted Karnivan knights with torches," Dathan said, in disbelief. "And they're coming here."

"This can only mean one thing," Melzar said quietly. "Akbar knows who you are and he brought them here. Quick, to the forest! We haven't a second to lose!"

Chapter Nine

Like four phantoms in the night, Melzar and his young charges fled from the farmhouse and dashed around the corner. "Stay low," Melzar urged. "Run to the grape arbor. From there perhaps we can make it to the forest."

"Sir, the barn is closer," Dathan suggested.

"They'll search there first," the farmer replied. "Our best refuge is the grape arbor."

Sterling was in the lead and he dropped to one knee as he reached the back corner of the house. A line of blazing torches marked the edge of the woods. "More Karnivans," he said, with fear in his voice.

"They have us surrounded!" Dathan cried.

"Stay low and run to the grape arbor," Melzar ordered. "It's our only chance."

"Sir, what about the dogs?"

"Nay," Melzar said firmly. "They stay here. Miriam will care for them when she returns. Now run!"

Twenty terrifying seconds later, all four fugitives lay shrouded in grape vines as a score of Karnivan knights came thundering across the farmyard. It was a moment of sheer terror. Dark silhouettes swept swiftly toward them like phantoms of death and destruction. Thundering hooves pounded the earth. Blazing torches cast an eerie, pulsating light and reflected from polished armor. Lying on the ground beside Lanna, Dathan felt the pounding of his own heart and struggled to breathe. He reached out—his sister was trembling.

Holding their torches high, the soldiers swept past the arbor without seeing the fugitives and rode down upon the little farmhouse. Another line of torches swept around from the front of the house and Dathan realized that the Karnivans had surrounded the building. "Stay low, but run," Melzar urged. "Head straight for the forest! Once they discover that we're not in the house, they'll come searching for us."

Leaving their hiding place in the arbor, the four fugitives ran frantically for the safety of the forest. Just as they reached the tree line, two mounted knights with blazing torches abruptly appeared from ambush behind a huge oak. "Halt!" they cried, leveling crossbows at the four terrified figures. "One move and you're dead!"

Sterling sprang forward and Dathan saw, to his amazement, that he had his stave from the skirmish. The youth almost seemed to fly as he leaped upward toward the nearest horse, swinging the stave with all his might and knocking the knight from his saddle. His companion turned, saw what Sterling had done, and swung his crossbow toward the boy.

Melzar's sword was in his hand. As the Karnivan knight aimed his crossbow at Sterling, Melzar raised his sword over his head and hurled it with all his might. Like an arrow from a longbow, the missile sped true to its target, penetrating the knight's chain mail and burying itself in the man's chest.

The Karnivan's eyes grew wide as he realized that he was mortally wounded. With a gasp of agony he turned and fired his crossbow and then abruptly tumbled from the saddle. The deadly bolt from the crossbow struck Melzar squarely in the chest.

As Dathan and Lanna watched in horror, Melzar gripped the bolt with both hands. Grimacing with pain, he pulled the projectile from his body and dropped it in the grass. His legs trembled as he stepped to the dead Karnivan soldier and removed his sword. With the magnificent weapon in his hand once more, he collapsed upon the ground.

"Melzar!" Dathan cried. Stunned, he threw himself upon his knees beside the form of his friend.

The dying farmer struggled to breathe. "Go...on," he gasped, grimacing in pain and forming each word with great effort. "Go to...Ainranon. The...book..."

Dathan leaned closer and suddenly realized that Lanna and Sterling were beside him. "What is he saying?" Lanna asked.

"The...book will...guide you," Melzar gasped. With great effort, he raised both hands and the young people saw that he was holding a book bound in black leather. "The book..." The old man's head fell back and his breath rattled in his throat. The book sank back to his chest. His eyes closed, and Dathan feared that he was gone. But then his eyes opened once more and he looked directly at Dathan. "I...give you...book." Gasping for breath, he raised the book again. His lips were moving, but no sound was coming forth. "...guide you." With these words, he closed his eyes and was gone.

"Melzar!" Lanna cried, sobbing. "Dathan, he's dead."

Dathan's eyes blurred with tears.

Shouted commands echoed across the farmyard and the trio looked back to see torches moving toward the barn. "We have to run for it," Sterling said urgently. "Quick! Where is Melzar's sword?"

"He had it in his hands when he collapsed," Dathan replied. "It has to be right here."

Hurriedly, all three searched in the darkness. "Where's the other Karn?" Dathan asked Sterling.

"This was his last raid," Sterling replied, and Dathan knew what he meant.

"The Karnivans are coming this way," Lanna reported, with terror in her voice.

Dathan looked up. Nearly two dozen torches swept across the yard as the soldiers searched for them. "Come on," Sterling urged. "We don't have time to find the sword. We have to get out of here!"

Dathan pulled the book from Melzar's grasp. "Good-bye, my friend," he said softly. "You have helped me greatly. I shall miss your friendship and your counsel."

Sorrow enveloped Lanna, Dathan, and Sterling like a cloud as they arose and turned to the safety of the forest. Although they had sheltered at the farm for little more than a fortnight, Melzar and Miriam had become dear friends to them, and the sudden loss of the gregarious farmer weighed heavily on each of them. For Dathan, the blow was greatest, for he had spent the most time with the old man. He had not only lost a friend, for Melzar was not just a farmer. The master swordsman had become Dathan's mentor.

The moon came out at that instant, full and bright, and bathed the landscape in its silvery beams. It was just enough for the Karnivans to see the fugitives. "There they are!" a voice shouted. "After them!"

Terrified, the three young people dashed between the trees of the forest. Limbs and briars tore at their arms and faces in the darkness, and the sounds of thundering hooves and angry shouts added to their terror. "Stay together!" Dathan called. "Follow Sterling!"

Suddenly, a new sound added to their fears: the deadly

zing! of arrows and bolts. The soldiers were shooting at them. Sterling darted and dodged through the trees, running for all he was worth. Enough moonlight trickled through the trees to allow Lanna and Dathan to keep him in sight, yet they struggled to keep up with him. They ran until their lungs burned. Finally, Sterling paused for breath, head down, with his hands on his knees. The twins caught up, panting and gasping for breath.

Panting heavily, Sterling held up one hand. “Listen,” he gasped. Dathan and Lanna held still, listening intently while they struggled to catch their breath. The noises of their pursuers had faded away, and the only sounds they heard were the chirrup of a tree frog and the hoot of a distant owl.

“We’ve lost them for the moment,” Sterling said, “but we’ve got to keep moving. They know we’re in here and they’ll have the woods surrounded before long.”

Even as he spoke they heard a shout and then saw the glow of torches among the trees. “Look!” Dathan cried. “They’re coming from the other direction—they already have us surrounded!”

Sterling leaped to his feet. “We’ve got to keep moving. Follow me. Perhaps if we head more to the west we can circle around them.” More torches appeared, bobbing among the trees like blazing fireflies, and the forest echoed with Karnivans shouting directions and orders. Sterling stopped for a moment, surveyed the situation, and then took off in a different direction. The fugitives ran until their sides ached and their lungs screamed for air. Sterling stopped again, and the twins leaned against each other, trying desperately to suck enough air into their tortured lungs.

“It’s no use running,” the Judan youth panted. “They have us surrounded. If we keep going like this we’ll run right into them. We've got to hole up and hide, but it has to be an exceptionally good place. They're going to scour these woods until they find us."

Dathan pushed his way through a dense thicket to reach Sterling. His foot suddenly broke through a layer of dirt and leaves and he found himself falling into empty blackness. As he fell, his head struck a projection of rock. He saw an intense flash of white light and then all was darkness and silence.

"Dathan," Lanna called softly, "where are you?"

There was no answer.

Sterling turned around. "What..."

"Dathan's gone," she told him.

Sterling glanced around. "What do you mean, gone?"

"He just vanished! He was just here, right between you and me, but now he's gone!"

Sterling looked irritated. "Dathan! Dathan! Where are you?" He worked his way back toward Lanna. Moments later, he gave a startled exclamation. "There's an opening in the ground beneath the thicket!" Ducking into the thicket, he disappeared from view.

Lanna waited anxiously.

"Lanna! Crawl under the thicket!"

Lanna looked around in confusion. "Sterling, where are you?"

"Dathan fell into some sort of cavern," Sterling replied. "Crawl under the thicket and I'll guide you to it."

"I can't see you."

"Aye, but I can see your feet. Crawl under the bushes and I'll guide you to me. But hurry, for the Karnivans will be here shortly."

Lanna dropped to her knees and crawled into the thicket. At that moment half a dozen Karnivans rode up and reined to a stop less than ten yards away. Their blazing torches lit the area with a pulsing amber glow. Lanna hugged the ground, not daring to breathe.

"They came this way," a rough voice said. "They have to be close. Dismount and search the area. Look under every log; search every thicket and windfall. They came this way and we're going to find them." Lanna's heart pounded with terror.

"Lanna!" Sterling's whisper cut through Lanna's fear and confusion. Moving only her eyes, she scanned the darkness beneath the thicket and saw Sterling's hand beckoning to her. "Crawl toward me, but be quiet," Sterling mouthed the words silently. Lanna nodded and started toward him.

The space beneath the thicket grew brighter and she looked up to see two torches hovering directly over her hiding place. Two Karnivan knights were standing less than three paces from her and preparing to search the thicket! Terrified, she looked at Sterling for direction. He held up one hand as a signal for her to lie still. She nodded and dropped her face to the ground, covering her head with her arm.

The crackling of branches and the shuffling of leaves told her that the soldiers were coming closer. Terrified, she could only wait. Her heart pounded so loudly she was sure that the Karnivans would hear it. She held her breath, trembling with terror. After several heart-stopping moments, the soldiers moved on. Weak with relief, Lanna let out her breath in a long, sobbing sigh. Never before had she known such terror.

"Lanna!" Sterling's whisper caught her attention and she lifted her head. "Crawl toward me, but quietly!"

Moments later she was right beside him.

"Dathan fell into some sort of cavern," Sterling told her again, whispering so low that she could barely hear him, though his lips were almost touching her ear. "I'll guide you to it. Slide your legs in first, and then climb down carefully. I have no idea yet how deep it is, but we have to hurry before the soldiers come back. Can you do it?"

Wordlessly, she nodded.

Sterling took one of her hands and guided it to a narrow crevasse in the ground. Moving quickly but as quietly as possible, she slid her legs into the opening. "Wait," Sterling told her. "Let me go first. I'll guide you down." Lanna pulled her legs out of the crevasse and Sterling scooted over in her place and slid into the opening. In the darkness it looked as if the ground had swallowed him.

"All right, come on down," Sterling's whisper came a moment later. "I'm right below you. It's only about eight feet deep."

"Is Dathan all right?" Lanna asked.

"I don't know yet. Come on down. I'll guide your feet."

With Sterling's help and directions, Lanna slid into the crevasse and climbed safely down into the cavern. The underground chamber was dark, with just enough light for Lanna to make out Sterling's silhouette. Just then a low, unearthly groan sounded at their feet, and Lanna jumped in fright. "What was that?"

"It's your brother," Sterling replied, kneeling and then feeling about in the darkness until he found the form of Dathan. "Here he is."

Dathan was lying on his side, silent and unmoving. Lanna dropped to her knees beside him. "Dathan! Are you all right?"

Dathan rolled over on his back and his eyes opened. "What... what happened?"

"Just lie still," Sterling told him. "You'll be all right."

"Where—where are we?"

"You fell into some sort of cavern. We're down here with you."

"Dathan, are you all right?" Lanna was nearly beside herself with worry.

"My head...hurts," Dathan said slowly. Abruptly, he tried to sit up. "The Karns! Where are the Karns?"

"I think we're safe in here," Sterling reassured him. "Lie still. I don't think they'll find us here."

"Unless they walk through the same thicket we did," Dathan interjected.

"I believe that your brother is going to be all right," Sterling told Lanna, to her great relief.

The girl looked around the dim recesses of the cavern. "It sure is dark down here. I wish we had a light."

"We'll have to get used to it," Sterling told her. "I think we're going to be down here for quite awhile. We dare not leave until the Karnivans abandon their search."

"How long do you think that will be?" the girl quavered.

"Maybe several days," Sterling ventured.

"Several days!" Lanna was aghast.

"Maybe we could walk out," Dathan suggested. "Caves like this sometimes go for miles and miles. If we came out of the ground several miles from here, we would escape the Karns."

"We dare not risk it in the darkness," Sterling told him. "There could be drop-offs. Or we could simply get so lost that we'd never find our way out."

"Keep searching!" a rough voice called just then, and the three fugitives lapsed into silence. They listened tentatively as the Karnivan knights searched for them, calling to each other and cursing the futility of their search. "Keep searching!" the rough voice called again, and the trio realized that he must be the Karnivan captain. "They have to be in here! None of you are leaving this forest until you find them!"

After several minutes, the voices and sounds of activity faded away and the fugitives knew that the searchers had moved on to other parts of the forest. Dathan sat up, rubbing his head as he did. "That was scary."

Sterling moved closer to him. "How are you feeling?"

"My head feels like it got kicked by a mule, but other than that, I'm fine."

Sterling's knee brushed against an object and he reached down and touched it. "Melzar's book! You brought it with you."

"I suppose it fell in with me," Dathan replied with a chuckle. "May I have it?"

"Sure." As Sterling passed the book to his friend, the volume fell open and Lanna gave an exclamation of surprise. "Look! Look at the book! It's glowing!"

Dathan held the book in both hands as all three stared at it. Just as Lanna had said, a faint glow of white light emanated from the pages of Melzar's book. As they watched, the volume glowed brighter and brighter until the underground chamber radiated with an intense white light. "Incredible!" Sterling whispered.

The three fugitives sat in silence for a moment or two, staring in fascination at the glowing book. Dathan closed the volume and the light vanished immediately. When he reopened it, the pages began to glow again, glowing brighter and brighter until the cavern once again blazed with light. Lanna reverently touched the page. "This could light our way through the cavern," she suggested.

Sterling's eyes widened. "It certainly could! If the light continues to shine, perhaps the book could take us all the way to another opening. This could allow us to evade the Karnivans."

"We should mark some sort of trail as we go," Dathan suggested. "If we can't find another way out, we could at least find this place again."

Sterling nodded. "Good thinking."

"I think we should spend the night right here," Lanna remarked. "It's dark outside—we wouldn't see an opening if we found one. If we wait until morning, the daylight would help us find another entrance."

"Melzar was saying that the book would guide us," Dathan said quietly, turning the pages of the book as he did. "I wonder what he meant."

"The light will enable us to see our way," Lanna replied. "Without it, we would be walking in total darkness. That's what he meant."

Dathan shrugged. "Perhaps."

Sterling frowned. "I'd sure like to know what happened to Melzar's sword. We could use it if we come face to face with the Karnivans."

"He had it," Dathan told him. "I know he did! I saw him pull it from the body of the Karn soldier. But then, when he collapsed, it wasn't there!" He swallowed hard. "I'm sure going to miss him."

"He was a real friend," Sterling interjected.

"Miriam was too," Lanna replied.

Dathan propped the book open against a rock so that its light continued to illuminate the cavern. Without realizing it, he sat staring at Sterling until the other youth noticed. "What's the matter?"

Dathan blinked. "Before we go any further, don't you think it's time you told us the whole story? Melzar told me to ask you."

Sterling stared at him blankly. "The whole story? What are you talking about?"

"It seems that half of the Karnivan army is pursuing us," Dathan told him. "You told us that you are Judan, but there has to be more to it than that. Grimlor would never send this many troops just to capture one Judan youth. Come on—what have you done that makes the Karnivans so determined to find you?"

The Judan youth sat silent for several long moments. At last, he took a deep breath and let it out in a long sigh. "All right. I suppose it's only fair. And I must admit—you both have proven yourselves as loyal friends." With these words, he reached inside his boot and withdrew an object, which he laid on the rocky floor of the cave. "There. That's what the Karnivans are after."

Dathan and Lanna stared. "That's it? Why would the Karns be after that?"

On the floor lay a moldy leather case. Nearly ten inches long, it was slender, barely two inches in width. The case was worn and dirty and looked as if it might fall apart at any minute. "That's it?" Dathan was incredulous. "Why would the Karns be so anxious to get their hands on that?"

Sterling smiled mysteriously. "Wait until you see what's inside."

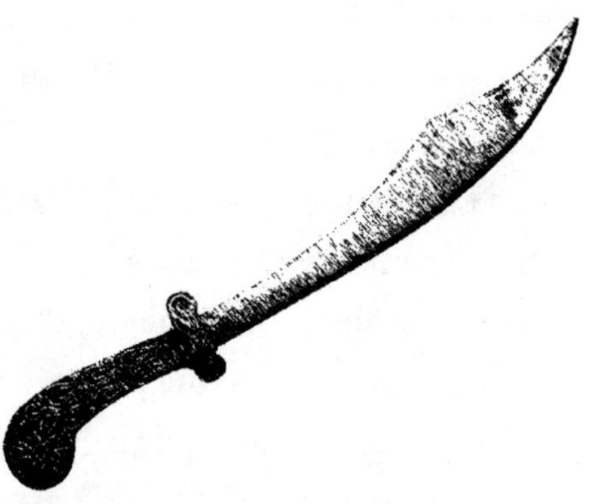

Chapter Ten

Safely hidden from the Karnivan knights who searched for them so relentlessly, the three fugitives sat on the rocky floor of the cavern. Lanna and Dathan studied the strange leather case before them. "The Karns are after that?" Dathan asked again. "What could be so important about that?"

Sterling shrugged. "This is why they're pursuing us."

"So they're really after this sheath or whatever it is, and not after you?"

Sterling smiled. "So it would seem."

"Let's just give them the sheath, and then perhaps they'll quit chasing you," Lanna suggested.

The Judan boy shook his head. "It's not that simple. I'm afraid that they'd still kill us or take us captive, with or without this."

Lanna eyed the object. "Why is this so important?" Lanna asked.

"Give me half a chance and I'll tell you," Sterling said with a smile.

Dathan touched the old leather case. "It's grimy and oily," he said with disgust, wrinkling his nose and rubbing his fingers together as if to rid them of some noxious substance. "What's in it?"

Sterling picked up the leather case, opened it, and took out a lustrous golden dagger. "This is why the Karnivans pursue us so relentlessly," he said quietly.

The twins studied the gleaming weapon. Made of solid gold, it had an ornate handle engraved with intricate symbols and set with three lustrous sapphires. The blade, thin and delicate, was slightly curved and tapered to a fine point. In the darkness of the cavern the golden dagger seemed to glow with a light of its own. "Where did you get that?" Dathan asked in awe. "It must be worth a fortune!"

Lanna gazed at Sterling with a look of wonder. "Are you a prince?"

The Judan youth laughed. "If you two will quit peppering me with questions, I can tell the story behind the dagger." He handed the treasure to Dathan. "Here."

Sterling shifted position, leaned back on his elbows, and began his story. "My father is the Marquis of Marden, a small shire in northern Cheswold. For many years he and the Duke of Marden have been close personal friends. The duke's castle is less than fifteen miles from ours.

"Late one night, my father roused me from a sound sleep and instructed me to dress quickly. 'Father,' I asked, 'what is wrong?'

" 'Just dress and prepare to follow me in silence,' he whispered. He was extremely troubled about something—I could see it in his face. As soon as I was dressed, he motioned me to follow him and then led me to the highest tower in the castle. When we came out on the sentry walk, I could see that the night was dark, without moon or stars. 'What are we doing here?' I started to ask, but he shushed me before I could get the words out."

Sterling paused, and Dathan could see that he was struggling with his emotions.

"Father carefully checked to be sure that we had not been followed, and then turned to me with a look of sorrow. 'My son, I may never see you again,' he said, and I stared at him in shock. 'Listen carefully,' he told me, 'for we may not have much time.' He leaned over the battlements and studied the darkness below as if to check for signs of pursuit.

"Once he was satisfied that all was well, he turned back to me. 'Son,' he said to me, 'I fear that I must lay a responsibility upon you that is far greater than any father should ever place upon a son.' He then handed me the dagger. 'You must guard this with your life. If this should ever fall into the hands of the enemy, disaster such as we cannot imagine would fall upon Cheswold. As you love your country, son, swear to me that you will never yield this to the Karnivans.'

"I gave him my pledge," Sterling told Dathan and Lanna, "and he then told me the significance of the golden dagger."

"Why is the dagger so important?" Dathan asked. "I'm sure it must be valuable, but why would so many knights be pursuing us to get it?"

"The crown jewels of Cheswold were lost to the Karnivans in a raid nearly fourteen years ago," Sterling explained. "King William was killed and his infant son and daughter were taken. To this day, no one in Cheswold knows where the crown jewels are, or where the royal heirs are. If the prince is still alive, he would be the rightful king of Cheswold."

"Do you think he might still be alive?" Dathan asked.

Sterling shrugged. "No one knows. If he is, he would be just about our age. His name is Eristan."

"How old would the princess be?" Lanna asked.

Sterling shrugged again. "I'm not sure. I think she was a little younger, but still pretty close to the same age." He cleared his throat and then resumed his tale. "The only part of the crown jewels the raiders didn't get was this royal dagger. If they gain possession of the dagger, I think they can lay claim to the throne of Cheswold."

"Meaning that Grimlor would rule Cheswold?" Dathan asked in alarm.

"Aye. And that would be unthinkable." Sterling clenched his fists in determination. "For that reason, the dagger must never fall into their hands. I will give my life before I will let them have it."

He frowned as he recalled the fateful night. "'For more than a decade,' my father told me, 'the golden dagger of Marden has been secreted in the keep at the duke's castle. No one in all of Cheswold knew it was there except the duke and King Vladimir. When the duke became aware of an assassination plot on his life, he delivered the dagger to my possession for safekeeping.'

"My father gazed at me, and I will never forget the look in his eyes. 'Son,' he said, 'what I am about to tell you will place your life in jeopardy, and yet I must tell you for the sake of your quest. King Vladimir seems content to allow the Karnivans to encroach upon Cheswold and he has made no plans to attempt to drive them out. For several months, the Duke of Marden, the Duke of Leeds, and I have been planning a counter attack to drive Grimlor and the Karnivans from Cheswold once and for all. We have been sending our most trusted men throughout the shires to gather a secret army and launch a surprise assault on Grimlor's armies.'

Sterling sighed. "Father's countenance was sad as he told me, 'Tonight the duke has sent me word that some of my most trusted men are planning an attempt on my life. He could not tell me which men, only that the assassins are among my best. He instructed me to place the dagger in the hands of one that

I could trust; and that one is to try to carry the dagger to Ainranon. Son, that trusted one is you. Tonight, I know not whom else I can trust.'"

Sterling's face was grave as he continued. "I promised my father that I would give my life to protect the dagger, and that I would do my best to carry it safely to Ainranon."

Dathan nodded.

" 'May King Emmanuel himself protect you, my son,'" Father told me, and for the first time in my life, I saw tears in his eyes. He hugged me, and then gave instructions that I was to leave immediately. We descended the stairs to the sentry walk on the inner curtain wall, and that's where it happened. We heard a cough from the shadows, and Father drew his sword and challenged the unseen enemy. One of the sentries stepped into the light, and we could tell by the look in his eyes that he had heard everything. He drew his sword, and he and Father fought. Just when Father was winning, four more sentries came running, but we had no way of knowing whose side they were on.

"Father grabbed me and said, 'Go out through the garbage port and swim the moat. I have sent a signal, and someone will be waiting with your horse.'"

"Your horse?" Dathan echoed.

Sterling nodded. "A servant had slipped my horse from the stables two days earlier in preparation for this very eventuality, yet I had not even missed him."

"What happened in the fight on the wall?" Lanna interrupted, wide-eyed.

"I wanted to stay and help Father in the battle, but he insisted that I go. As I ran for the garbage port in the outer curtain wall, I saw several knights come to Father's aid. The last thing I saw of my father, he and those loyal knights were battling for their lives. I do not know if Father is alive or dead."

Dathan felt a chill go up his back.

"I left the castle through the garbage port as Father had instructed and swam across the moat. Just as Father had promised, a servant was waiting for me. I took my horse, Victor, and rode south as hard as I could go without killing him. After three days of hard travel, the Karnivans caught up with me just outside your castle. You know the rest."

Sterling glanced down at the golden dagger in Dathan's hands. "And now you know why the Karnivans are pursuing us so relentlessly and why the dagger must never fall into their hands."

Dathan turned the dagger over and then handed it back to Sterling, who carefully placed it back within the moldy sheath. "That's the most incredible thing I ever saw," Dathan said quietly.

"It's absolutely beautiful," Lanna remarked.

"Well, it's more than beautiful," her brother told her, "it's the symbol of the throne of Cheswold. Like Sterling, we must pledge our lives to make sure that this never falls into the hands of Grimlor."

Sterling placed the dagger in his boot once again. "I would suggest that we spend the night right here— we're safe from the Karnivans. In the morning, we can see if we can find another entrance to the cave. Unless I'm mistaken, our pursuers will spend the next two or three days searching this region of the forest and I'm afraid we'd be captured the moment we emerged from the opening above us."

Dathan agreed. "As soon as you two are settled for the night, I'll close the book so that the light will go out." Moments later, when all three fugitives were ready, Dathan closed the book. The darkness was so intense it was almost terrifying.

Dathan awoke the next morning and rolled over, wondering why his bed seemed so hard. He sat up, rubbing his eyes and waiting for them to adjust to the dim light. He frowned in bewilderment. He could see just enough to make out the indistinct forms of unusual rock formations. As far as he could see in either direction, curtains and walls and arches and passageways stretched before him, all crafted from stone. A faint trickle of light came from somewhere overhead, though he couldn't see the source. He shook his head, trying to make sense of it all. It was as though he was inside some bizarre sort of castle.

The cave! Suddenly it all came back, and his consciousness sharpened. He and Lanna and Sterling were fleeing from the Karnivans, and they had spent the night underground. He sat up. Sure enough, his sister was to his right, sound asleep on the rocky floor. To his left, Sterling was just waking up.

Dathan stretched and yawned, and Sterling opened his eyes. "Time to get moving, sluggard," Dathan said, teasing his friend. "I've been waiting for hours for you to wake up!"

Sterling sat up and stretched and then gave Dathan a friendly grin. "I suppose you have breakfast ready, then?"

"Just finished," Dathan said, with a laugh. "Sorry you missed it."

Their conversation woke Lanna and she sat up groggily. "Breakfast? Where's breakfast?" She looked around the dark recesses of the cavern eagerly.

"Your brother ate it all," Sterling told her with a straight face.

"Dathan!" Lanna was upset. "Dathan, how could you? We're hungry, too, and—" By now she was awake enough to take a look around and realize where they were. "Oh. There was no breakfast, was there?"

Dathan gave her an understanding smile. "Not yet, Lanna. But if we can find our way out of here, perhaps Sterling can set some of those snares he's so famous for. And then maybe he could provide a rabbit or two for breakfast."

Sterling laughed. "If you two are ready, let's see if we can find a second entrance to this cavern. If we can find our way out, I'll see what I can do with the snares."

Dathan picked up the book and opened it. Within moments, the cavern glowed with a brilliant white light. Dathan studied the cavern. They were standing in the center of a long, narrow chamber which stretched out of sight in both directions. Overhead, huge crystalline stalactites hung from the rocky ceiling like giant chandeliers. Dathan looked to Sterling for direction. "Which way?"

His friend took a deep breath and then pointed. "Let's go in that direction."

"Wait. We were going to mark our trail," Lanna reminded her companions.

"You're right, Lanna," Dathan told his sister. "Thanks."

"I'll be right back," Sterling promised, and began to climb toward the entrance that had admitted them to the cave. Within moments he was back with a long stick. "We'll use this. Dathan, why don't you lead the way? You have the book for light."

And so they set off through a confusing maze of dark corridors, vast underground chambers, and twisting passageways, with Dathan in the lead and Sterling bringing up the rear with his stick, carefully marking their trail in the event that they had to retrace their steps. The book in Dathan's hands blazed brightly, lighting each subterranean chamber with intense light that not only enabled them to see their way but also brought courage and cheer.

"I'm thankful that we have Melzar's book," Lanna observed, after the first few moments of travel. "Without it we couldn't see a thing!"

"If the light goes out, we will be in serious trouble," Sterling replied.

Moments later, the narrow corridor they were traversing opened into an immense, vaulted chamber, and Dathan paused in astonishment. "Oh, my! Look at this!"

Before them stretched a vast, glittering treasure vault of indescribable beauty and splendor. As they entered, the immense room suddenly flashed with color and light. The walls and ceiling of the vast underground chamber shimmered with dazzling color and sparkled with tiny pinpoints of twinkling light. Dathan stepped close to the wall to see millions of tiny crystals sparkling with fiery colors. He realized that they were reflecting the brilliant light from Melzar's book. High overhead, huge crystalline formations glowed with a light all their own. The chamber was enormous, extending for several hundred paces in each direction, with a vaulted, crystalline ceiling nearly two hundred feet above their heads. They had entered a vast cathedral of breath-taking grandeur and beauty.

"I've never seen anything like it," Lanna said in a whisper, awed by the splendor surrounding her. "How do you suppose that it got here?"

"King Emmanuel created it, of course," Sterling replied, surveying the breath-taking scene with wonder. "To suppose that it got here by any other means would be the height of absurdity."

"Look," Dathan said, pointing. "That may very well be the most beautiful part of all. Water!" Flowing through the center of the vast chamber was a crystal stream of pure water. The three travelers lost no time quenching their thirst. They then spent the next few minutes exploring the vast chamber and wondering at its incredible beauty. Reluctantly, they left the grandeur of the magnificent room and resumed their journey.

Half an hour later, Lanna asked, "how far have we come?"

"Not that far, I'm afraid," Sterling replied. "Maybe a little less than a mile."

"Less than a mile?" the girl echoed. "It seems that we have been walking forever!"

Sterling paused and glanced back at the darkness behind them. "Hey, wait! Look behind us!"

"What is it?" the twins said together as they turned around.

Sterling pointed. "There. Up toward the ceiling—do you see a speck of light?"

Lanna and Dathan stared in the direction that Sterling indicated. "I don't see anything," Lanna ventured.

"Let me close the book so we can see better," Dathan suggested, and abruptly did so. Immediately, the cavern was plunged into intense darkness.

"I see it!" Lanna said, nearly shouting. "There's a ray of white light coming down from the ceiling!"

"It may be another entrance to the cavern," Sterling said quietly. "Let's check it out."

The chamber was filled with boulders nearly as big as houses and the travelers found that by climbing from one to another they could reach the source of light. Just as Sterling predicted, it turned out to be a small opening through which they could pass. One by one they slipped through to find themselves on the side of a forested hill. The autumn leaves were ablaze with color, and a thick layer of fallen leaves carpeted the hillside. "We did it!" Lanna exulted. "We—"

Sterling clapped a hand over her mouth. "Quiet!" he

whispered in her ear. "The Karnivans may be close by!" When she nodded to show that she understood, he removed his hand from her mouth. "I'm sorry to do that," he told her quietly, "but we can't take a chance on the enemy hearing us."

"I wasn't thinking," she said, embarrassed. "I was just so glad to get out of that cave... out into daylight!"

Sterling nodded. "I understand."

"Get down!" Dathan whispered urgently. "Soldiers!"

The frightened trio dropped to the ground in the thick carpet of autumn leaves. As they watched, two mounted knights rode slowly through the valley below, carefully surveying the hillsides above them. It was easy to identify them. "Karnivans!" Sterling spat out.

"And you know who they're searching for," Dathan remarked.

"So we know it's not safe to come out here," Sterling told the others. He looked at Lanna. "I guess it's back to the cavern. Sorry."

Lanna smiled. "You won't get any complaints out of me," she replied. "Better to face the cavern than the Karnivans."

They slipped back into the darkness of the cavern as silently as phantoms. Dathan opened the book and the cavern blazed with light as they carefully made their way back down to the cavern floor and continued their trek through the underground labyrinth. The hours passed, and just as Lanna complained that she couldn't go another step, Sterling spotted another window of daylight. To reach the opening, they had to traverse an extremely difficult and treacherous chimney climb, but after nearly half an hour of arduous effort, they emerged from the darkness to find themselves on a rocky hillside shrouded with evergreens. Below them was a wide, peaceful valley through which flowed a slow moving river. Along the eastern bank of the river ran a narrow, rutted lane. The trio crouched in the shade of a tall fir, silently surveying the landscape before them for any signs of the enemy. Sterling alternated between studying his map and watching for enemy knights.

"I don't see any signs of the Karnivans," Sterling said at last. "I think we should travel tonight. If we wait another half hour until it's nearly dark, we can follow the road fairly safely. If anyone approaches, we can take to the forest or the bushes until they pass. We'll have a half moon, so it won't be totally dark, but that will be safer than if we had a full moon. What do you think?"

"I think I'm hungry," Lanna replied.

"We both are," Sterling reminded her. "Dathan didn't share his breakfast, remember?"

"You were going to snare a rabbit, remember?" Dathan teased.

"You're both making me hungry," Sterling complained, half in seriousness and half in jest. "Let's talk about something else."

The rising sun cast its ruby rays over the eastern hills as three travelers stumbled down a gentle slope, tired and hungry. Sterling had insisted that they travel most of the night, and had finally consented to stopping for three hours of sleep just before daybreak. Just now they found themselves approaching a small village.

"I sure would like to stop for breakfast at an inn," Dathan sighed with a yawn. "I'm so hungry I could eat a whole hart and so tired I could sleep for a week!"

Sterling stopped in the roadway and turned to face him. "I think you have a good idea, my friend. Let's do it!"

Dathan snorted. "And what would we use for money?"

Sterling stared at him. "My father is a marquis—do you think he would send me penniless on a quest such as this?"

It was Dathan's turn to stare. "You're serious about stopping here, aren't you?"

"Of course."

"Oh, dear, do you think it's safe?" Lanna asked with a worried frown.

Sterling nodded. "I think we can do it with little risk of discovery. I figure we're more than thirty miles now from Melzar's farm."

The twins were overjoyed. "I'm going to eat until next Tuesday without stopping," Dathan declared. "See if I don't!"

Sterling grinned. "You think you can afford that since my father is paying for it?"

Dathan shrugged. "To be honest, I wasn't thinking about the money; I was thinking about the food!"

Five minutes later they approached the front door of an ivy-covered inn, stepping around two stacks of lumber placed close to the door. "Watch out for that plank," Lanna said, pointing to a long beam standing on end. "It looks like it could topple over at any moment and crush someone."

"They must be doing some work on the building," Dathan commented.

"Aye, but you would think they would stack their lumber a little further from the door. Who wants to climb over beams and planks just to get inside?"

"If anyone asks any questions, keep quiet and let me do the talking," Sterling instructed his companions. "It will be safer that way."

"Do you expect any trouble?" Dathan asked quietly.

"Nay, but it's best to be prepared." With a broad smile, he opened the door. "Sweet cakes and creamery butter, here I come!"

The proprietor of the inn led them to a table in the dining salon. "It is an honor to have you with us today, sire," he said to Sterling, bowing low as he spoke.

"Thank you, sir," Sterling responded. He turned to the twins. "Order as much as you want. You deserve it, and we have no idea what lies ahead."

"We have a rich venison stew, sire, accompanied by the most excellent fritters and fruit jellies. In addition, our chef has prepared the finest trout..."

"Bring us three full orders of all of it," Sterling ordered. "We've been traveling a bit this morning and we're quite hungry and tired."

The proprietor bowed. "Of course, sire. Right away, sire. And how is your father, sire?"

"I haven't been home in a few days, my good man," Sterling replied. "I trust that he is well."

"As do I, sire." Bowing low, the man hurried away.

Dathan stared at Sterling. "He seems to know you. And he asked about your father. Do you know him?"

"Father and I lodged here last year on a hunting trip," Sterling replied. "We were with His Majesty at the time, I believe."

Lanna was amazed. "You went hunting with the King of Cheswold?"

Sterling shrugged. "Father knows him well."

The meal came in mere minutes and the hungry travelers began to eat ravenously. "Don't look too eager," Sterling cautioned his companions. "We don't want to draw undue attention to ourselves."

Just as they were finishing the delicious meal, Sterling glanced toward the door of the inn and an expression of sheer panic crossed his face. Dathan leaned close without turning to look. "What is it?" he whispered.

"Turn around slowly and take a brief look at the men who just entered," Sterling said in a low voice. "Tell me who they are."

Dathan's heart pounded furiously as he slowly craned his neck to take a glance at the door. As he did, his heart seemed to stop. Terror swept over him. Standing just inside the door with six of his men was Sir Keidric, the lord of Windstone Castle!

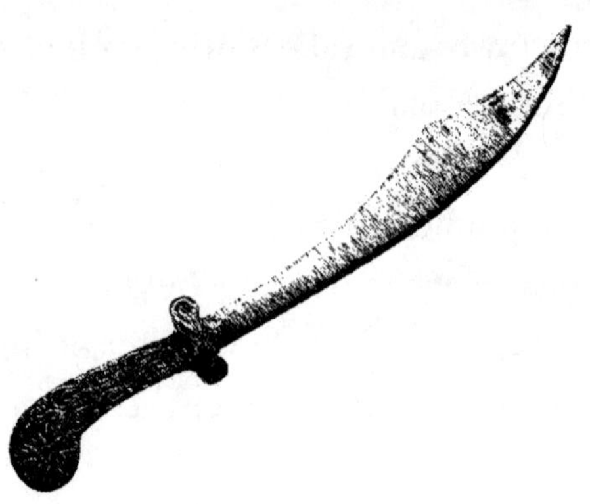

Chapter Eleven

"Who is that?" Sterling asked in a whisper as he stared at the knights by the door.

Dathan was shaking so badly he could hardly maintain his balance at the table. His heart constricted with fear and the blood pounded in his head. Darkness swam before his eyes and he felt dizzy and nauseous. He struggled to breathe.

"Who is that?" Sterling asked again.

"We're as good as dead," Dathan croaked. "That's Lord Keidric."

Sterling's face tightened. "That's what I feared." He ducked his head. "Stay still. He's looking this way."

Dathan saw Sterling's eyes widen slightly and his heart lurched. "What's he doing?"

"They're coming this way."

Fear swept over Dathan and Lanna in waves. They trembled uncontrollably. The twins were runaway slaves, and their master, the very man who could order their death, was in the room with them! Sterling saw the terror in their eyes. "Relax," he said quietly. "You're just slaves to him; he doesn't even know you. He won't recognize you! Did you not tell me that you had only seen him once?"

"What are they doing?" Dathan demanded. His voice trembled.

"Sir Keidric is about to pass our table in a moment," Sterling whispered. "Don't look at him; just look at your food until he passes."

Dathan lowered his eyes and forced himself to look at his plate. He took a deep breath. He would not look at Lord Keidric as he passed. As long as Lord Keidric did not notice him, everything would be fine. He would not look...

The seconds seemed like hours. Tension filled the air. Dathan held his breath. Would Lord Keidric never pass their table? Finally, when he could take it no longer, Dathan lifted his head and looked up.

It was the wrong moment. Sir Keidric and his men had already passed the table and were striding toward a table in the corner of the salon, and, just at the moment that Dathan glanced at them, the master threw a quick glance over his shoulder. Their eyes met. Dathan looked away quickly, but it was too late. In that one brief moment, Sir Keidric recognized him. He spun around. "Dathan?"

Terrified, Dathan leaped to his feet. "Run, Lanna!" He turned and bolted for the door and to his amazement saw that his sister was already ahead of him. Sterling darted around the table and rushed to catch up.

"Dathan!" Sir Keidric shouted. "Wait!" He and his men raced for the door.

Sterling grabbed a chair as he passed it and hurled it behind him at Sir Keidric. The nobleman tried to sidestep the tumbling chair, but he was too late. With a crash he fell to the floor with two of his men on top of him, buying the fleeing fugitives several seconds of precious time.

Lanna wrenched open the door of the inn and darted through with Dathan and Sterling right on her heels. Sterling slammed the door. He had the presence of mind to grab the beam outside the door and hurl it to the ground behind the stacks of lumber, thus effectively barring the door. Lanna and Dathan stood still, paralyzed with fear. "Run!" Sterling shouted. "Run to the forest!"

The door of the inn suddenly shook as the men inside attempted to open it. A barrage of blows struck the door. "Run!" Sterling shouted again.

The frightened trio dashed for the forest directly across from the inn. Sterling led the way, darting around trees and dodging branches as he ran for his life. The twins were right behind him. The slope was extremely steep, and they struggled for breath as they climbed. When they came to a deep ravine, Sterling spun around for a quick check on their pursuers.

As the fugitives watched through a narrow break in the trees, they saw the seven men come dashing around the side of the inn. For several moments the men stood in the middle of the roadway, looking in all directions. Failing to find their quarry, they made their way to the door and stood for a moment or two inspecting Sterling's work before moving the heavy beam to one side.

Sterling was relieved. "They're not pursuing us," he happily told his companions. "Stop and catch your breath."

"This is just great," Dathan puffed. "You have half the Karnivan army pursuing you and wanting to kill us all, and Lanna and I have Lord Keidric pursuing us and wanting to kill us. Is there nobody on our side?"

"We can't lose them again," Sir Keidric's voice floated up to them. "We've chased them... find them before... all the... to Ainranon." The three fugitives could only catch snatches of the conversation, but what they were hearing was frightening.

Dathan looked at Sterling in alarm. "They know we're traveling to Ainranon!"

Sterling sighed. "I heard that."

"What are we going to do? If they know we're running to Ainranon, they'll pursue us the entire way!"

Sterling held up one hand. "Listen!"

"We can't let them..." Sir Keidric was speaking again, and they strained to hear his words. "...find them..." His voice was low and indistinct again for several seconds and they lost his words, but what they heard next caused them to shrink back in fear. "...capture them and kill them!"

Dathan glanced at Sterling, who held up his hand for silence.

"Search the village... the mountain... to find... not get away..." The men moved out of earshot and their words were lost altogether.

Lanna gripped Dathan's arm. "Would Lord Keidric really kill us if he catches us?"

Dathan grimaced. "It sounds as if he intends to, Lanna."

"What are we going to do?"

"We're going to make sure that they don't catch us," Sterling said fiercely. "We're going to make it safely to Ainranon! We're going to deliver the golden dagger to Lord Stratford!"

"That's all fine and good to say it," Dathan told him, "but talk is cheap. With Lord Keidric and his men searching for us and hundreds of Karns pursuing us, it won't be that easy!"

"We'll make it," the Judan youth insisted. "We have to! Cheswold is depending on us."

The trio traveled hard all that day. Avoiding the roads for fear of encountering the Karnivans or Sir Keidric and his men, they trekked through some desolate countryside, using Sterling's compass to follow a course that led directly south. The route that Sterling chose led them through one of the most scenic regions in all Terrestria, with sparkling streams, thundering waterfalls, and forests alive with the fiery colors of autumn, but the terrain was rugged and their progress was slow.

The sun was quickly dropping behind the steep mountain to the west as the weary travelers hiked down a leaf-carpeted slope and entered a secluded valley. A tiny stream meandered through the valley, laughing to itself as it tumbled along its rocky bed. On the slopes, the woods were vibrant with color. Fiery red maples, golden tamarack and birch, orange sugar maples, purple ash, and butter-yellow hickories all contrasted against the deep blue and green of the spruce and pines. A light breeze stirred in the treetops, causing the trees to moan and whisper to each other like old men watching a jousting tournament.

"Where are we to spend the night?" Lanna worried. "And what are we going to eat? I'm starving."

"We had a huge breakfast, remember?" Sterling jested. "That should hold you for a day or two."

"To be honest, I'm quite hungry, too," Dathan said.

"And we do need a place to spend the night," Lanna finished.

Sterling paused and looked around. "There's probably no better place than right here," he decided. "Dathan, why don't you and Lanna build a lean-to in that thick grove by the stream while I make and set some snares?"

"Sure," Dathan responded.

The twins worked their way down the valley gathering wood with which to build the lean-to and a fire. They had hardly gone a hundred yards when Lanna spotted a cottage in a clearing by the stream. "Look, Dathan, there's a house! Do you think it would be safe to ask them for food?"

Dathan studied the cottage. Smoke curled from the chimney, indicating that someone was probably home. Behind the little house was a small shed and a low building that he took to be a chicken coop. Except for one lone chicken that scratched about in the little yard of the secluded homestead, all was quiet and peaceful. Dathan hesitated. "I don't know, Lanna. We don't know who we can trust and who we can't."

"Let's see what Sterling says," Lanna suggested hopefully.

"Oh, so you trust his judgment more than you trust mine, huh?"

Lanna laughed. "He is the son of a marquis, you know. You're just a lowly slave. What do you know?" Lanna was teasing her brother, but she realized that he took it seriously when she saw the hurt expression on his face. "I'm sorry, Dathan. I was just jesting."

To her surprise, he grinned at her. "So was I. My problem is not that I'm a slave; my problem is that my only sister is a slave." He turned toward the head of the valley. "But you're right—let's see what Sterling thinks." Together they headed back to find the Judan youth.

"I don't know," Sterling said slowly, as he studied the little cabin a moment later. "We definitely could use some food, but we have to be careful who we ask. If these people are Karnivan sympathizers..."

"Who are they going to tell?" Dathan asked. "We're miles and miles from anywhere! This place is pretty secluded."

Sterling nodded. "It sounds like you're in favor of stopping and asking for food."

Dathan shrugged. "To be honest, I'm not sure what to think, but I can't say that I'm opposed to trying. I guess Lanna and I just want your opinion."

The Judan youth looked at the little cabin again. "Well," he said slowly, "you are right; it is secluded..."

At that moment the front door opened and a cheerful looking woman stepped out with a basket on her arm. As she closed the door, a series of high-pitched barks sounded from just inside. The peasant woman laughed and reopened the door. "All right, Freda," she told the little dog that came bouncing out after her, "you can help me gather the eggs. But you have to promise me that you won't aggravate the chickens."

The tiny dog responded with one sharp bark as if to make the promise, and the three travelers laughed. "What a cute little dog," Lanna remarked.

"I think we can trust this woman," Sterling decided. "Let's see if we can help her with some chores in exchange for a meal."

As Sterling approached the woman, the little dog ran in circles, barking and leaping into the air in her excitement. The peasant woman turned to see what was causing her little dog's reaction and her eyes widened when she saw the trio standing in the narrow lane that led to her cottage. "Well," she said in a friendly, motherly tone, "it seems that I have visitors. Welcome! To what do I owe the honor of this visit?"

"My good woman," Sterling said, "we are passing through on an extended journey and are in need of food and lodging. Might we do some chores around your place in exchange for a meal and a place to stay tonight?"

"You're welcome to stay, sire, and your friends as well. I'll be happy to feed you and shelter you."

"We thought we might help with some chores, ma'am," Dathan said, stepping forward. "Perhaps we can gather the eggs for you, milk your cow, and do any other work that needs done around the place."

A shadow seemed to cross the woman's face. "I have no cow,

though I did have a goat," she said darkly, "but the Karnivan raiders stole her. Perhaps someday I will have another."

"Perhaps we can do some other chores for you, ma'am," Lanna said hopefully.

"Darling, you and your friends are my guests," the woman told her. "I'll be happy to feed you and lodge you for the night. I would consider it an honor. Please don't feel as if you have to work to earn your keep."

Sterling glanced at Lanna and Dathan as if to say, "See? Didn't I tell you that this woman could be trusted?" He stepped forward and lifted the basket from her arm. "The least we can do is to gather the eggs for you."

The peasant woman smiled as she allowed him to take the basket. "I would be grateful, my lord. I'll be putting supper on while you do it." Her little dog ran around in tight circles, barking exuberantly and leaping into the air repeatedly as if to show her great delight with the arrangement.

"Dear, why don't you come into the house and help me start supper while your friends gather the eggs?" she said to Lanna. She turned to Dathan and Sterling. "Gathering the eggs is actually a game of treasure hunt," she told them. "The hens seem to find delight in laying their eggs in the hardest hiding places. I will give you a clue—you'll usually find most of them behind the house."

Dathan and Sterling headed for the back of the house. "She's a sweet old lady, isn't she?" Dathan said. "I'm thankful that we happened on this place."

"It will be good to get a good night's sleep and not worry about Sir Keidric or the Karnivans," Sterling agreed.

The boys spent the next ten minutes searching for the elusive eggs. Just as the woman had predicted, they found them in the most unusual places: in clumps of grass, under fallen limbs, inside a broken piece of pottery. Perhaps the most unusual of all was when Dathan found one egg four feet above the ground in the crotch of a persimmon tree. "How would a hen lay an egg up in a tree?" Dathan wondered aloud as he retrieved the egg.

"Why would a hen lay an egg in a tree?" Sterling responded.

Finally, they headed to the house with eleven eggs. As they entered the house, the little dog gave them a rousing welcome. "We found eleven," Sterling told the woman. "And you were right—the hens do seem to take delight in hiding them in odd places."

The woman laughed as she took the basket. "Thank you, sire. If you boys are hungry, you're just in time. Lanna and I just about have supper ready." When Dathan looked surprised at the use of Lanna's name, she said, "My name is Selma, by the way."

"I'm Dathan, and this is Sterling," Dathan told her. "We are grateful for your help."

"You're the ones the Karnivan knights are searching for," Selma replied, and for a moment or two, Dathan was so stunned that he was speechless.

"H-How do you know?" he finally managed. He looked accusingly at his sister. "Lanna?"

"I-I didn't say anything," Lanna replied, and it was obvious from her facial expression that she was just as shocked at the woman's statement as her brother.

Sterling stepped forward, and he was visibly shaken as he took Selma's hands in his. "My good woman, please tell us," he implored. "How do you know who we are?"

Selma laughed. "Don't fret, my friends. Your secret is safe with me. The Karnivans will never know that you were here."

"But how do you know who we are?"

The woman's face seemed to darken with anger. "Those murderous Karnivans came through here two days ago like a plague on horseback," she answered. "Said they were looking for three young criminals, two young men and a woman, and then searched my place like it belonged to them! Didn't ask my leave or nothing! They had the audacity to go through my house, scattering my things right and left. It took me half a day to clean up the mess after they were gone."

"And you guessed who we were when you saw us today?" Dathan was amazed.

"I knew it as soon as I laid eyes on you," she said sweetly. "What have you done to get the Karnivans so stirred up?"

"It's a long story, ma'am," Sterling told her.

She laughed. "I suppose it's best if I know as little as possible anyway. Well, find a place at my little table and we'll put the vittles on."

The friendly old woman fed them well, placing steaming bowls of stew and thick slices of brown bread before them and then refilling their bowls as fast as they emptied them. As they ate she talked nonstop, asking them questions, offering snippets of advice, and entertaining them with funny stories from her childhood. By the time they finished the simple meal, they felt as if they had known her for years. "My good woman," Sterling told her as he wiped away tears of laughter at the conclusion of one of her stories, "our visit with you has done us a world of good. I've laughed more tonight than I have since I started on this quest."

"It's been good for me too, Sterling," she assured him. "A body does get lonely from time to time." She sighed. "I do have Freda, but I also find myself longing for human companionship. It's good to have you here."

She glanced at Lanna. "Would you like more cider, dear?"

Lanna shook her head. "No, ma'am. And thank you."

Selma leaned across the table with a serious expression on her kind face. "May I offer you three a word of advice?"

"We're listening," Sterling told her.

"The Karnivans are searching everywhere, and they're determined to find you. They gave me such an accurate description of you that I recognized you the moment I laid eyes on you. They even described your clothing in very accurate detail." She gazed at Sterling. "Your clothing in particular was a giveaway." She spread her hands as if to reason with them. "May I make a suggestion? You need to change into other clothes so that your pursuers don't recognize you so readily."

"Where would we find other clothes?" The question came from Lanna.

"I have some clothes from my husband and my sons before they passed on," she told them. "They're in a big trunk down in the cellar. If you three would bring the trunk up for me, we could go through the things together. I'm sure we could find some things that would fit."

"We're thankful for your help," Sterling told her. "Giving us your family items is a real sacrifice on your part, I am sure."

Selma smiled. "Anything to keep you from the clutches of those dreadful Karnivans, my dear."

She stood. "The trunk is heavy, and I'm sure it will take all three of you to heft it." She indicated the dinner table with a sweep of her hand. "I'll clean up later. Let's see what we can find for you to wear, shall we?" She lit a candle.

The trio followed her to a trapdoor in the floor. Handing the candle to Lanna, their hostess knelt and drew back two sturdy bolts. Dathan and Sterling struggled as they opened the door. "It sure is heavy," Dathan grunted.

"The trunk is in the back corner of the cellar," Selma told them as she balanced the heavy trapdoor on its hinges. "Bring it up here, would you?"

Lanna went first, holding the candle high as she descended the narrow stairs into the blackness of the cellar. Dathan and Sterling followed. To their surprise, the cellar was completely empty. "Selma," Sterling called, "where's the trunk? The cellar seems to be empty."

At that moment, the heavy cellar door came slamming down with a crash. The three startled young people heard the ominous sound of the two bolts being thrown. "Wait!" Sterling cried, dashing to the top of the stairs and throwing his shoulder against the unyielding door. "Selma, what are you doing?"

Selma's response was a burst of wicked laughter. Her words struck fear into the hearts of the fugitives. "The Karnivans are offering a generous reward for your capture," she told them. "I will have my goat, after all!"

Chapter Twelve

"Don't do this to us!" Sterling cried, slamming his shoulder repeatedly against the sturdy trapdoor. "You don't know what you're doing!"

"I know very well what I'm doing," came the old woman's muffled answer through the thickness of the door. "I'm preparing to buy a goat."

Suddenly the darkness of the cellar seemed to close in about the three young captives, stifling and choking them. The flickering candle struggled to dispel the inky blackness, and Lanna's hands trembled as she held it. Evil was in the room with them; they could feel its presence. Fear wrapped its cold fingers around their hearts. Lanna began to sob. Dathan stepped close and wrapped his arms around her.

"I have money," Sterling bargained. "Release us, and I will pay you more than the Karnivans are offering."

"You have no idea how much they are offering," Selma chortled. "Believe me, lad, they are being quite generous. I will buy a dozen goats if I like."

"You can't trust the Karnivans," he replied, attempting to reason with her. "They will never come through on their promises."

“Then that will be my problem, not yours,” the old woman replied with a wicked laugh.

Dathan dashed to the top of the stairs. “Please, let us out,” he begged. “The Karnivans will kill us if you turn us over to them.”

“And that is your problem, not mine.” The words were cold and heartless.

“But we trusted you!” Dathan was nearly in tears.

“That also is your problem, not mine.” Footsteps sounded on the floor above their heads. Seconds later, to their horror, the three captives heard the sound of the front door opening and then closing again.

“She’s going for the Karns!” Dathan told the others in disbelief. “She’s actually going to do it!”

Lanna was sobbing. “How can she do this to us? She seemed so kind, so loving, so... generous. She reminds me of a grandmother.”

“She was planning this all along,” Sterling said grimly. “We walked right into a trap!”

“And now they’re going to...to kill us!” Lanna was sobbing so hard she could hardly talk. Dathan slipped down the stairs and held her close.

“Not if we can find a way to escape,” Sterling replied fiercely. “Come on, Dathan, help me look. There has to be a way out of here.”

Two hours later, the three terrified captives watched as the stump of the candle dissolved in a puddle of melted wax. The wick floated on top, burning with a feeble blue flame. At last, to their great dismay it flickered and went out, plunging them into inky darkness. There would be no escape. Dathan trembled as he opened his book, allowing the glowing pages to illuminate the cellar.

A number of hours later, Dathan awoke to the muffled sound of horses' hoof beats and the stamping of human feet. He raised his head, but all was darkness. The sound of gruff voices filtered slowly through the fog of his consciousness. Somewhere above him, a door opened, and he heard voices. He yawned sleepily. *Why don't they just go back to sleep?* he thought drowsily.

Terror slammed down upon him as memory sharpened abruptly. Selma had trapped them in her cellar. The voices above him were the voices of Karnivan knights coming to take them captive! Sterling's quest for Ainranon was about to end in failure. The golden dagger was about to fall into the hands of the enemy.

In his terror, he heard the sound of the bolts being drawn. Abruptly, the trapdoor was flung open and lamplight splashed upon the stairs, blinding in its intensity. He sat up. "Lanna! Sterling!"

To Dathan's astonishment, Sterling dashed up the narrow stairs and hurled himself upon the enemy. "You won't take us alive!" he screamed. The sounds of a struggle followed.

Lanna's hand upon Dathan's neck frightened him. "What shall we do, Dathan?"

"Run for it," Dathan responded grimly. He dashed up the stairs, hoping that his sister would know to follow him.

The twins burst through the trapdoor and into a scene of horror. The room was filled with Karnivan knights in armor, and Sterling was fighting for his life. Barehanded against ten armed men, he thrashed and struggled and fought, striking out with his fists, slamming his slender body against armored bodies. In his frenzy, he managed to send three or four of them tumbling. "You'll never take us alive!" he screamed again.

Dathan felt the cold edge of a sword against his neck, and a harsh voice rang out, "Yield, knave, or your friend dies! Right now!"

And just like that, the long flight was over. Knowing that resistance was futile and that further struggle would bring death to his friend, Sterling quit fighting. A burly Karnivan knight brought a gauntleted fist down against the back of Sterling's head and the valiant young man crumpled to the floor, unconscious. The three captives were quickly bound, carried from the house, and thrown across the saddles of huge warhorses. The burly Karnivan knights were nearly beside themselves with glee as they lashed their quarry to the horses.

After a tortuous ride of nearly an hour, the cavalcade of Karnivan soldiers rode with their captives into a dense forest. "Wait till Captain sees what we brought him," a rough voice exulted, and Dathan realized that it was the first time that any of the Karnivans had spoken since leaving the little cottage in the woods. "Men, each of us is almost guaranteed a promotion! Extra rations and grog, at the very least!"

The horses came to a halt, and Dathan was relieved when the painful bouncing stopped. Rough hands quickly untied him and then dragged him from the saddle, allowing him to fall to the forest floor. He was thankful for the thick carpet of leaves that broke his fall. Standing to his feet, he turned to see Lanna and Sterling close by. His sister's expression was one of terror, while the Judan youth wore a look of defiance.

"Come." Their captors marched them quickly through the woods toward a series of flickering amber lights. As they drew nearer Dathan was amazed to see that they were entering an enormous Karnivan encampment. Campfires and tents stretched among the trees as far as the eye could see.

After a trek of two or three minutes, the captives were halted in front of a large tent. A burly Karnivan officer sat upon a tree stump eating a meal beside a roaring campfire. He looked up at their approach. "Are they who I think they are?"

"Aye, Captain," the leader of the knights said with a satisfied grin. "At last we've caught the little vermin we have pursued so long."

The captain looked the trio over briefly and then focused his attention on Sterling. "Give me the dagger."

Sterling looked defiant. "I don't know what you're talking about."

The captain glanced at one of the soldiers, who stepped in front of Sterling and slugged him in the gut. The youth bent over in pain, struggling to catch his breath. "I'll ask you again, knave. Give me the dagger."

"I-I don't have any d-dagger," Sterling grunted through gritted teeth, trying desperately to draw a breath.

The Karnivan captain shrugged. "You have a choice. Either give me the dagger, or we take off your heads and then simply take the dagger from your dead body. We'll start with the girl."

Sterling's expression showed that he was struggling. Even though he knew that resistance was futile, his commitment to his father kept him from simply handing the golden weapon to the enemy. Defiance glittered in his eyes, and Dathan winced. Sterling's resistance would get them all killed. "Do it, Sterling," he whispered.

Sterling glanced at him, and Dathan saw the hopelessness that was in his eyes. "It wasn't supposed to end this way, Dathan. What will my father say?"

"You did your best, my friend," Dathan assured him. "Your father could not ask for more than that, nor could he ask for a braver son. But he would not have you die for something that is beyond your reach."

Sterling sighed and nodded. He glared at the Karnivan captain. "Untie my hands. I'll give you the dagger."

Dathan feared that Sterling would attempt to resist when his hands were untied, but the valiant youth simply reached down into his boot and withdrew the moldy sheath. With a sigh of resignation and a defiant look on his face, he handed it to the captain. "Thus our quest ends in failure," he said quietly to Dathan and Lanna.

The Karnivan captain studied the grimy object with disdain for several long moments and then opened it. A look of delight spread across his rugged features at the first sight of the lustrous golden dagger. With a sneer of triumph, he tossed the sheath back toward Sterling, who stooped and picked it up. His shoulders sagged as he tucked the grimy object back into his boot.

"We have what we sought," the captain said. "Kill them."

Dathan stiffened with fear. He glanced at Lanna and saw that her eyes were filled with terror. Sterling seemed unperturbed by the command. "Your orders, sir, were to bring us back alive."

The Karnivan officer shrugged. "We have the dagger. That's all we were after. I don't have the patience to mess with three prisoners."

"Take us to Grimlor," Sterling demanded. "I have a message for him."

The captain's eyes narrowed. "What is your message?"

The daring youth shook his head. "The message is for his ears alone. Kill us and he never receives the message."

"We'll torture it out of you," the burly Karnivan threatened. "We'll start with the girl."

"Sir, I would be very careful how you handle this entire matter," Sterling replied with a sternness that amazed Dathan. "Everything that happens here tonight will get back to Grimlor, and you and I both know that. If you're not careful, sir, he'll have your head. Handle the matter correctly and there's a huge promotion in it for you." He fixed the officer with an unflinching stare.

The captain laughed nervously. "You're a feisty one, aren't you?" He turned to one of the knights who had made the capture. "Tie them securely to a tree, out of my sight. I want a double guard on them."

"Aye, sir." The knights led the three captives away through the trees to a large oak and then tied them securely with their hands behind them and their backs to the tree. Two knights were assigned to guard them. The area was brightly lit by a large bonfire that leaped and danced less than ten paces from the tree. There would be no chance of escape. Lanna began to sob again.

The Karnivan guards strolled away eight or ten paces and began to chat. "You saved our lives," Dathan told Sterling, with an admiring glance.

Sterling shrugged despondently. "Does it really matter now, Dathan? The dagger is in the hands of the Karnivans. Our quest ended in failure."

Exhausted from the ordeal, all three young captives fell asleep quickly.

Dathan awoke. He slowly opened his eyes and risked a glance at the guards. The two Karnivans stood chatting with each other eight or ten paces away. From time to time they glanced in the direction of their three captives. Disappointed, Dathan closed his eyes again. If the guards were this alert and watched them this closely, there was no use even thinking about an escape attempt.

He sensed or heard a slight noise and opened his eyes. The night was warm, yet a cold chill swept over him. Something of great significance was about to take place. He could feel it. Moving only his eyes, he carefully scanned the area. All was quiet except for the two guards.

He heard the tiniest whisper of sound and turned from the fire, staring in fascination as he saw an ethereal figure shrouded in white. He blinked, rubbed his eyes sleepily, and looked again. The figure was gone now, but he was sure he had seen an old man moving silently through the trees, looking from side to side as if searching for something. He stared into the darkness for several long moments, but could see nothing out of the ordinary. He sighed. "Aye, it's been a long, hard day," he whispered aloud. "Time to get some sleep."

He stared. The old man had reappeared and was striding slowly, silently through the camp. To Dathan's astonishment, the apparition was looking directly at him and moving straight toward the oak tree. As he watched, the strange visitor strolled right past the two guards, but they paid him no attention whatever. Dathan's heart pounded. Who was this midnight visitor?

The mysterious old man approached him slowly, carefully, almost as if taking great care not to frighten him. His eyes were friendly and he smiled when he saw Dathan watching him. Dathan held his breath. The old man stopped in front of the oak and knelt before him. He was so close that the startled youth could have reached out and touched him.

Dathan gasped as the old man drew a knife. He opened his mouth to call for help, but no words came out. Sterling and

Lanna were both asleep and the guards were busy talking. With his hands tied behind, Dathan was helpless to defend himself against the old man. Rigid with fear, he could only wait.

Chapter Thirteen

The mysterious visitor raised the knife, and Dathan drew back in fear. The man saw the terror in his eyes and lowered the knife. "Dathan," he said softly, "do not be afraid. I have not come to harm you."

"Sire, who are you?" Dathan started to ask, but the old man quickly held up one hand, silencing him. "Do not speak, lad, for the guards cannot hear me, but they can hear you. I have been sent to help you."

Dathan nodded slightly to show that he understood.

Dathan studied the knife in the old man's hands and then began to relax. This mysterious visitor meant him no harm—he could see the concern written in his eyes. As the youth watched, spellbound, the old man used the knife to free him from his bonds. When the last of the ropes had been cut away, the old man said quietly, "Do not move until I have freed the others. You do not want to call attention to yourself." Dathan nodded slightly.

As the old man moved toward Lanna, Dathan glanced at the two Karnivans guards, who still stood talking a few paces away. As he watched, one of the men turned and looked straight at the tree. Dathan held his breath. Their benefactor was about to be discovered! To his great astonishment, the guard turned back to his companion and resumed his conversation. Dathan stared at the guard. Could the Karnivan knights not see the old man kneeling beneath the oak?

Turning his attention from the guards, he watched as the mysterious visitor carefully cut Lanna's bonds, freeing her completely. He did it so gently, so carefully, that the girl never awakened. When she was free, the old man then freed Sterling without waking him.

"Be patient, lad, and stay still. This will take but a moment longer."

The old man reached out and gently touched Lanna's arm. "Lanna, dear, wake up, but keep quiet. Lanna, wake up." Lanna's eyes opened and then grew wide with fright as she saw the old man, but he gently covered her mouth with one hand and told her softly, "Lanna, do not cry out. I am here to help you. Do you understand?" Wide-eyed, the girl nodded. "Good," the old man said, and removed his hand from her mouth. "Lanna, please stay perfectly still as I wake Sterling. Will you do that? Just nod your head slightly to show that you understand."

Lanna complied. She glanced at the Karnivan guards and then back again, and her eyes were wide as she settled her gaze on the mysterious visitor. The old man moved over to Sterling and soon had him awake.

"Now listen closely, you three," the ethereal visitor told them in a low voice. "Do not move until I give the signal. When I create a loud diversion, crawl slowly around the base of this tree until you are on the opposite side. Even though you will be tempted to do so, do not move quickly, for you will simply call attention to yourselves. When you are behind the tree, stand to your feet and walk directly away from here, being careful to keep the tree between you and the fire. Again, walk, but do not run. If you move too quickly, you will call attention to yourselves. Stay together and keep walking until I catch up to you."

He took a moment to smile reassuringly at each of them. "You have doubts as to the feasibility of my plan—I can see it in your eyes. If you will follow my instructions and remember to move slowly and deliberately, two minutes from now you will be free of this dread place. I guarantee it."

The old man glanced at the two guards and then turned back to the three speechless young people. "I know what I am doing. Trust me. King Emmanuel has sent me to free you. Remember, do not move until I create a very loud diversion. The moment you hear it, crawl one by one around to the back side of the tree." He smiled again. "Ready? I'll see you again in about a minute."

As they watched, wide-eyed, the old man stood quickly to his feet and walked boldly past the two guards, who paid him no attention. Stepping close to the fire, he reached inside the breast of his long, flowing robe and withdrew several items. Turning his head to give the three astonished fugitives a broad wink, he then tossed the items one by one into the blazing fire.

Immediately there was a loud explosion, and the raging fire was hurled in all directions. The guards, standing less than five paces from the bonfire, were knocked to the ground by the force of the blast. Momentarily stunned, they shook their heads and stood shakily to their feet. At that moment, several more explosions hurled the men to the ground again. When the last of the explosions had taken place, the two guards stood warily to their feet once more. One of them glanced toward the oak tree, turned away, and then groggily realized that his prisoners were missing. As he opened his mouth to tell his companion, yet another round of explosions took place, and he hurled himself to the ground of his own accord.

The blasts rocked the camp, awakening every soul within hearing, but also creating pandemonium and confusion. Karnivan knights ran in all directions, some crying out in fear. Officers cursed and shouted orders, which simply added to the chaos and confusion. When at last some of the more level-headed knights figured out where the explosions had come from, all they could find were several small fires burning profusely and two disoriented guards who had no idea what had happened to their prisoners.

Following the old man's instructions to the letter, Dathan, Lanna, and Sterling had waited until the explosions started and then crawled behind the huge oak tree. Though tempted to stay and watch the fireworks, they immediately set off through the woods, being careful to walk in a straight line directly away from the bonfire. At last they paused at the edge of a dense thicket which blocked their path. "Which way do we go?" Dathan asked aloud.

"I'm not sure," Sterling replied, searching for a path in the darkness but finding nothing. "Perhaps we should try to crawl under it."

"Well done, my friends," a quiet voice said, and the old man appeared in the darkness. "Follow me, but there is no need for haste. By the time the Karnivans pick up your trail, we will be long gone."

"Sire, what did you throw in the fire?" Sterling asked, tugging at the old man's sleeve. "That was incredible."

"Karwac root," the old man answered shortly. "It grows far underground and explodes when it comes in contact with heat." He grinned at Sterling. "We're not in a panic, but we really don't have time for questions, either. Follow me. There will be plenty of time for questions later."

"Sire, that was excellent," Dathan told the old man, as he and his companions finished a meal of roast corn, potatoes, and pheasant. They were sitting on stumps around an open campfire at the edge of a wide meadow. Overhead, the stars glittered like diamonds in a velvet sky. "There's nothing like a meal cooked over an open fire."

The old man smiled as he leaned over, picked up a piece of firewood, and then added it to the fire. Thousands of brilliant orange sparks flew upward. "I knew that you would be hungry after all that you have been through today."

"Who are you, sire?" Sterling asked. "How did you do what you did tonight? How did you know that we had been taken captive by the Karnivans?"

"My name is Wisdom, or Sir Wisdom, as some call me. I am the servant and personal counselor to King Emmanuel. His Majesty sent me to rescue you."

Sterling studied the old man. "You say that you are a servant, yet your clothing identifies you as nobility. Which are you—a nobleman or a servant?"

"Aye, I am a nobleman, Sterling, yet I take no delight in title or position," Sir Wisdom answered quietly. "My greatest title is that of servant to the King."

Lanna stared at Sir Wisdom in awe. "Did King Emmanuel really send you to rescue us from the Karnivans?"

The old nobleman shook his head. "I didn't rescue you from the Karnivans. I rescued you from yourselves."

"What do you mean, sire?"

"You three are on a quest to save Cheswold from the Karnivans, for in delivering the golden dagger to Lord Stratford you will help keep Grimlor's armies from taking over. In reality, your quest is for King Emmanuel himself, and His Majesty has provided you with the means for success. Yet you have chosen to attempt to accomplish the King's quest in your own strength and in your own way."

All three young people leaned forward, puzzled by Sir Wisdom's statement. "We do not understand, sire," Sterling said quietly. "Please explain your words. How has Emmanuel provided for success on our quest? How are we attempting the quest in our own strength?"

The old nobleman turned to Sterling. "As you left on your journey, your father gave you a book. Where is it now?"

Sterling's face showed his bewilderment. "I-I do not know, sire. I do faintly remember my father giving me a book, but in the excitement of the moment I suppose I mislaid it. I have no idea where it is."

"That book was from King Emmanuel himself," Sir Wisdom explained. "There is no greater gift that a father can pass on to his son, and thus your father gave it to you. That book was to be the source of your success on this quest."

"And yet I do not even know where it is," Sterling lamented.

"Exactly." Sir Wisdom's voice was sharp but his eyes were gentle. "His Majesty's weapon of choice for you is the sword, yet you have neglected the sword and excelled in the use of the stave. His book was to be your guide on this extremely difficult and dangerous quest, yet you have not followed it—you have followed a handmade map and a compass rather than following the book that came from the King himself. You lied to the Karnivan captain in an attempt to avoid surrendering the dagger, rather than trusting Emmanuel.

"Sterling, you are a young man of incredible intelligence and ability, yet you are not to rely on those strengths. Rather, you are to rely on the strength and wisdom of your King. You are skilled with the stave, to be sure, but the King's power is not in the stave. His power is in the sword."

He turned to Dathan. "And did not your friend Melzar give you a book? Yet you have not used it to guide you on this difficult journey."

Dathan drew Melzar's book from his tunic. "I do have it, sire. It fits comfortably into a fold in my tunic."

"And yet you have not allowed it to guide you and your companions. Why not? You and Lanna tend to follow Sterling, and that is only natural, for he is a born leader. And yet, Sterling is relying on his own abilities, and you two are relying on Sterling. My friends, you do not know what lies ahead on this quest, but I assure you, it will not be easy. You have not yet finished your journey across Cheswold and all of Karniva lies before you. May I remind you, Karniva is enemy territory? If you continue as you are, your quest will end in failure."

"It has already ended in failure," Sterling replied glumly as he drew the moldy sheath from his boot. "We lost the golden dagger to the Karnivans, sire. All we have left is this loathsome old sheath." He drew back his hand to toss the item into the campfire.

"Wait, lad!" Sir Wisdom's words stopped him just in time. "Do not destroy it."

Sterling looked at him in bewilderment. "Why not, sire? Without the dagger it is worthless."

"You were commissioned to deliver the golden dagger to Lord Stratford, were you not?"

"Aye. But the Karnivan captain now has the dagger. The sheath is worthless."

"Perhaps," the old man agreed. "But you do still have it. And it is a part of what you were given to deliver to Lord Stratford. You cannot deliver the dagger, but you can deliver the sheath. I would do that much."

"Without the dagger, our quest is a failure anyway," Sterling replied bitterly.

"Not if you have done your best and followed through on what is committed to your trust. True, the dagger is gone and cannot be recovered; and yet, you can still deliver the sheath. To fail to do so would be to fail in your quest."

Sterling frowned, thought about the nobleman's words for a moment, and then returned the sheath to its place inside his boot.

"You said that the book would guide us," Dathan said to Sir Wisdom. "How is that possible?"

Sir Wisdom stared at him. "Did not Melzar teach you that?"

"Nay, sire. He taught me the use of the sword, but he did not teach me how to use the book. I have his book, but I do not have his sword, though we searched diligently for it."

The old man began to laugh. "Dathan, Dathan. Aye, lad, you do have his sword. You hold it in your hand at this very moment."

Confused, Dathan looked down at his hands. "Begging your pardon, sire, but I do not have Melzar's sword. All I have is his book."

Sir Wisdom leaned forward. "Give me his book." As Dathan placed the leather-bound book in his hand, the old nobleman stood to his feet. Gripping the book, he drew it back and then brought it down swiftly in front of him. In an instant, the book was transformed into a gleaming sword.

Dathan recognized the magnificent weapon instantly. "Melzar's sword!"

"Rather, it is King Emmanuel's sword," Sir Wisdom

corrected. He held the glittering weapon close to his side and immediately it became a book again.

Dathan was stunned. "I had Melzar's sword and didn't know it."

"The book is not only your defense against the enemy; it is your guide on this journey." Sir Wisdom handed the book to Dathan. "Open it. Let me show you what I mean."

Dathan did, and the pages of the book began to glow. "We have seen that the book provides light, sire, but how would it guide us?"

"Hold the book in front of you and turn in a slow circle," Sir Wisdom instructed. As Dathan followed the old man's direction, he noticed that the book glowed brightly when facing in one particular direction, but dimmed noticeably when facing in any other direction.

Dathan was fascinated. "What is it doing?"

"The book is showing you in which direction you should go. This is King Emmanuel's way of guiding you on this quest. If you follow the guidance of the book, it will lead you safely to Ainranon."

"We had a source of guidance and didn't even know it," Lanna said quietly.

"And yet there is more," Sir Wisdom replied. "Open the book to the last page." When Dathan complied he said, "Take the parchment that you find there." Within the book was a small parchment, and Dathan lifted it from the pages. "You may at any time send a message directly to the throne room of His Majesty," he told the trio, "by writing a message on the parchment, rolling it up, and releasing it. Emmanuel receives petitions from his children at any time, night or day. Whenever a need arises or you simply wish to speak to your King, send him a petition."

"That's incredible," Lanna said softly.

"As King Emmanuel's own child, you have the right to send him a petition at any time. Many of His Majesty's children do not make use of this incredible form of communication with their King, and yet it is their right and privilege."

"We need to use the book for guidance on the rest of our journey to Ainranon," Sterling observed. "And the petitions will be a source of strength and provision."

"Aye," Sir Wisdom agreed. "And one more thing: obey the voice of the dove."

"The dove?"

The old nobleman pointed upward. "Aye, the dove. Look above you."

The three young travelers looked upward. Perched in the branches overhead was a white dove of unusual beauty and grace. "He has been with you throughout this entire quest," Sir Wisdom told them, "though I have reason to believe that you were unaware of his presence. He will speak to you in a still, small voice which is easily unheard or ignored. Be careful to listen for his voice and to follow his counsel, for he will never lead you wrong. His counsel will always be in accord with the guidance of His Majesty's book. Obey the dove always and your quest will be successful."

Sir Wisdom glanced at the starry sky above them. "The hour is late, my friends, and you need your rest. Tomorrow I will teach you the proper use of the sword."

"I have one question," Sterling said. "Why did you rescue us in the manner that you did tonight? Was there not an easier way?"

The old man laughed. "Aye, for I could have simply walked up to the two guards and rendered them unconscious long enough for you to sneak out of camp. But it was more fun this way. The Karnivans are big, rough, and cruel, yet most of them are cowards at heart and they frighten easily. I love scaring them. Tonight I just had some merriment at their expense as I rescued you." Sterling and the twins laughed.

Sir Wisdom glanced at the dying campfire and then back at the young fugitives. "Tonight we shall sleep by the fire. I have prepared pallets for each of you. Tomorrow at first light I shall take you to my cabin, where I shall train you in the proper use of the sword."

Lanna looked around nervously. "Is it safe here? What if the Karnivans come?"

"You are very safe here," the old nobleman replied, "for the Karnivans can never find you. Rest well, my friends."

The glittering sword screamed through the air, sharp and deadly, and Dathan realized in that dreadful instant that he had made a tragic mistake. In his eagerness to attack, he had overextended himself, leaving an opening in his defense that his opponent was now using to his own advantage. Desperately, Dathan threw himself to one side and the razor tip of the sword passed within two inches of his tunic. Dathan landed heavily, knocking the wind out of himself, but he immediately rolled and leaped to his feet with his sword extended.

His lungs screamed for air, but he dared not let his opponent know that he was winded. He feinted once with the sword and then took several quick steps to the left, circling the other swordsman. For a moment, he felt weak and dizzy as he struggled to draw a breath, but he kept his eyes focused on the sword that threatened him. At last, his diaphragm relaxed, enabling him to draw a breath, and the rush of cool air into his lungs was sweet and refreshing.

He studied his opponent. The other swordsman was taller than he, with exceptional reflexes and a swift sword. He exuded confidence. His footwork was sure and he seemed to anticipate Dathan's moves before he made them. Dathan could not afford another mistake.

Dathan feinted once more to the left and then immediately brought his sword around in a slashing backhanded cut, hoping to catch the other swordsman off guard. But his blade merely glanced harmlessly off the shoulder of his opponent's chain mail shirt. In the next instant Dathan found himself retreating hastily as he desperately parried a ferocious barrage of cuts, slices, and combinations. The deadly sword seemed to strike with the swiftness of lightning, hammering relentlessly away at his feeble defenses until his breath came in ragged gasps and there was no strength left in his sword arm. Thoroughly exhausted, he fought back desperately, but it was no use. The fight would soon be over, and there would be no reprieve. He knew how it would end.

And then it happened. Completely spent and struggling just to maintain his balance, he stumbled and went down on one knee. He raised his sword in a last-second effort to protect his head, but he was too late. Mercilessly, the glittering sword of his opponent came slashing down.

Chapter Fourteen

Sterling's sword flashed like silver lightning as he brought it down with all his strength, striking Dathan's chain mail shirt just above the collar bone. The force of the blow sent Dathan sprawling in the grass. He hit face-first, dropping his sword as he fell. For a moment he lay perfectly still, drawing in deep breaths and gathering strength. "You don't have to kill me to win," he said without raising his head.

Lanna turned on Sterling in fury. "What were you trying to do?" she demanded hotly. "It did indeed look like you were trying to kill him! He's your friend, remember? If you've already forgotten, Sir Champion Swordsman, Dathan is the one who rescued you from the dungeon at Windstone Castle! If it weren't for him, you'd be dead right now, or in the hands of Grimlor."

The Judan youth lowered his sword. "I'm sorry, Lanna." He extended a hand to Dathan. "Let me help you up."

Lanna wasn't finished. "Why did you hit him so hard? This is just training. You acted as if Dathan was your worst enemy!"

Sterling winced and turned to face her. "Lanna, I'm sorry."

The girl glared at him. "Well, next time don't hit him so hard. I hope he takes your head off in the next skirmish."

"Lanna, simmer down," Sir Wisdom told the girl quietly, as he moved toward the combatants. "Sterling shouldn't have struck so hard once he had the clear advantage, but remember, Dathan and Sterling are fighting with the swords given them from Emmanuel. His Majesty's sword will inflict no injury upon a true son or daughter of the King. That is why they could practice so ferociously upon each other without danger of causing harm."

Lanna took a deep breath and let it out slowly. "I'm sorry, Sterling."

Sterling helped Dathan up and then grinned at Lanna. "If I ever get the upper hand again, I'll try to remember to go easy on him."

She wrinkled her nose at him. "I do think he owes you one good lick, though."

Sir Wisdom put his gnarled hands on the shoulders of the two weary young men. "Let's take a break from the swordplay, shall we? You both look like you could use some rest. Lanna, bring the water pitcher from the house, would you? We can sit in the shade of that oak while we discuss what you did right and what went wrong..."

Dathan and Sterling had completed nearly a week of intensive training in a secluded mountaintop meadow under the expert tutelage of the aging nobleman. Both youth had marveled at the speed, strength, agility, and skill of the old man, and they quickly realized that, like Melzar, he was a master swordsman. In an incredibly short period of time he had taught them skills of the sword as no one else in all Terrestria could have done.

Panting with exertion, Dathan sank to his knees in the tall grass beneath the oak. "I think my whole body hurts," he said with a laugh. "I've never been so tired in my life."

"You're not the only one," Sterling replied. "I feel like I've been fighting for a month without stopping."

"A drink and a brief rest will do you both good," Sir Wisdom told them as he took a seat beneath the tree. "I must say, lads, that you fought well. You've learned quickly, and your skills are improving rapidly. You are true knights of His Majesty."

Lanna appeared with the pitcher of water and four earthenware mugs and began to serve the liquid refreshment.

"Dathan," the sword master said, "fight in the strength of your King. You wield his sword; battle in his power! At first you did, and you drove Sterling before you, in spite of his exceptional speed and skill. But then, when Sterling counterattacked you panicked and began to fight in your own strength. I saw the moment it happened, and it was at that moment that you began to lose. Always remember, His Majesty's strength is your strength if you trust in him."

Dathan dropped his head.

"Look at me, lad." Dathan raised his eyes and returned Sir Wisdom's gaze.

"You are exhausted, are you not? Are you not at this moment so weary that you feel as if you could not fight if your very life depended on it?"

"Right now I'm so weary," the youth confessed, "that I don't think I could even pick up my sword."

"The flesh grows weary in the battle," the old man said kindly, "but he who battles in the strength of Emmanuel will renew his strength. As His Majesty has promised, he shall run and not be weary; he shall walk, and not faint. Dathan, draw your strength in battle from the heart of your King."

He turned and looked at the Judan youth. "Sterling, you have the same weakness as Dathan: you battle in your own strength, though in a far different manner. You are a natural swordsman if I ever saw one. Your reflexes are swift; your footwork is superb; and you almost seem to be able to read your opponent's mind. Yet your great ability is your weakness, for you tend to trust in yourself and your own abilities, rather than trusting in the power of your King. Like Dathan, you fight as if the battle depends on you."

He looked from one young swordsman to the other. "Lads, I can teach you all the right moves with the sword. I can teach you the importance of footwork, how to study your opponent, how to counter any move he makes, when to advance and when to retreat; but the most important lesson is this: always battle in the strength of your King. You wield his sword; you must battle in his power."

Three days later, Sir Wisdom and his three young guests sat around a small table enjoying breakfast together. Dathan gazed around the little cabin as if to fix the scene firmly in his memory. "We're going to miss you, sire," he said to the nobleman. "Like Melzar, you have helped us tremendously. Without your help, we would never make it to Ainranon."

"Aye, and I shall miss you, my friends, for I have greatly enjoyed your company and your fellowship," Sir Wisdom replied, "but time is of the essence and you must get to Lord Stratford as quickly as possible."

"Does it really matter now?" Sterling muttered. "The golden dagger is gone forever."

"Aye, it does matter," the host said quietly. "True, the dagger is in the hands of the Karnivans and it seems to you that your quest must end in failure. But rest assured that you have not failed. Sterling, there is more to this journey than even you realize." He stood up. "Before you go, I have a gift for each of you—well, for Lanna and Sterling." With these words, he handed a leather-bound book to Lanna. "Your sword, my lady.

As Melzar told Dathan, it will guide you on your journey to Ainranon."

He then handed an identical book to Sterling. "The weapon with which you fight so well. In just ten days' time, my young friend, you have become very proficient with the sword and you are well on your way to becoming a master swordsman; but let me remind you that you must fight in the power of King Emmanuel. The arm of the flesh is weak and if you trust in your own skill, you will fail. His Majesty's power is limitless and will bring victory."

Sterling nodded. "I will remember."

"Dathan, you have the sword given to you by Melzar. I would tell you the same thing I told Sterling: fight in His Majesty's power, not in your own."

Dathan smiled. "I will remember, sire."

"Well, off with you, now," Sir Wisdom said, giving each of them a brief hug. "May King Emmanuel's love go with you and may his power always protect you. Follow the guidance of your book and the voice of the dove. And remember, make use of your right as children of the King to send petitions to the Golden City at any time."

As the three travelers stepped from the door of Sir Wisdom's cabin, Dathan looked up to see the beautiful white plumage of the dove in an elderberry tree directly overhead. "May we always follow your guidance," he whispered.

They traveled hard and fast for a number of days, always following the guidance of the book and listening for the voice of the dove. The miles fell away. Often they spent the nights in the forest, sleeping beside an open fire and dining on roots, berries, and small game that Sterling was able to trap in his snares. On occasion they stayed in homes or castles when assured by the book and the dove that it was safe to do so.

One afternoon after a particularly hard day of travel, they hiked over the crest of a ridge and saw a narrow lane winding its way down a gentle slope. "Shall we follow it?" Lanna suggested. "It does lead in the right direction and it would be much easier than trekking through the forest."

"Consult the book," Sterling prompted.

Dathan already had his book open. He studied the glowing pages for a moment. "The book says to follow it," he reported. The three travelers hurried down to the road and followed it to the south. When the road crested a steep ridge Lanna paused in the middle of the lane beside a tiny stream. "Oh, look," she said softly. "What a lovely place for a rest stop."

The road wound its way along a ridge overlooking a sapphire-blue lake guarded by tall stands of pine, poplar, and blue spruce. A gentle breeze whispered through the pines and scattered autumn leaves while a dancing sunbeam glittered and sparkled on the water, turning the mirror surface into acres and acres of shimmering blue diamonds. On the far side of the lake, a tiny cabin hugged a shoreline of pure white sand bordering a forest alive with the fiery colors of autumn. Overhead, a lone eagle with motionless wings rode the air currents in endless circles while fleecy clouds drifted lazily across the sky. The three travelers stood silently, transfixed by the panorama before them.

"May we stop for a few moments?" Lanna begged, gazing at the colorful reflections in the mirror of the lake. "This is one of the loveliest places I've ever seen."

"Why don't we stop for the night?" Sterling suggested, much to Lanna's delight. "I know it's a bit early, but I think all of us could use some extra rest."

"Sounds good to me," Dathan agreed.

"I'll set some snares if you two will build a fire," Sterling offered. "Be careful to build it smokeless as I showed you, for this ridge is quite exposed and we do not need to announce our presence." He pointed to a secluded area some fifty paces back from the crest of the ridge. "Let's build it back in that glen, right beside the stream."

Dathan helped Lanna start a tiny fire in the oak-shrouded glen and then paused for a moment to watch as Sterling set to work making half a dozen rabbit snares. The Judan youth knew the art of snare-making and was equally adept at placing his traps at key points along the trails and runways that the rabbits would use when they came out for their evening foraging. *We'll eat well tonight,* Dathan told himself as he went for more firewood. Sterling was a master at hunting small game and Dathan had no doubt he would be successful as usual.

He followed the stream down the slope toward the lake, choosing deadwood carefully as Sterling had taught him in order to build a fire that would emit almost no smoke. When he had an armload he hurried back up the ridge and dumped it on the ground beside the fire. "You're just in time," Lanna scolded in a friendly tone. "My little fire was about to starve for lack of fuel."

"Well, feed it all it wants but don't let it get too big," Dathan replied. "Sterling says we need to keep a low profile on this ridge." He watched for a moment or two as Lanna fed the wood into the fire in the precise way that Sterling had taught them. As planned, the fire gave off hardly a trace of smoke.

And then it happened. Lanna picked up the biggest branch and turned toward the fire with it, tripping over a broken limb in the process. As her brother watched in horror, Lanna fell headlong into the fire, throwing her hands up to protect her hair and face. With a scream, she rolled out of the flames.

Dathan was at her side in an instant, using his bare hands to slap out the bits of flame that lingered in her hair. He lifted her to her feet and looked her over anxiously. "Lanna! Are you all right?"

Lanna drew in a long, trembling breath. "I burned my hand."

Sterling was already pouring a double handful of cool water on the injured hand from the stream. When the water was gone he scooped another handful and did it again. "Let me see your hand."

Trembling, Lanna held out her right hand. Dathan winced when he saw it. The palm of Lanna's hand was an angry red and starting to blister. "It hurts, Dathan."

Dathan looked helplessly at Sterling. "What can we do for it?"

Sterling shook his head. "Not much, I'm afraid. I could make a poultice for it, but I have no idea where to find the right herbs." He flexed her hand gently, carefully studying her skin as the flesh moved. "It's not burned too deeply, but it is going to be quite painful." He grimaced. "I wish we knew where to find help."

"The book," Lanna suggested.

Dathan stared at her. "What about the book?"

The girl blinked back tears. "Perhaps it could guide us to someone who could help."

Dathan had his book open in an instant and began to turn it from side to side. He turned toward the west. "I think it's telling us to go this way." At that moment, the dove spread its snowy wings and glided in a long, gentle arc in that very direction.

Sterling looked at the twins. "Come on. Follow the dove."

Ten minutes later the dove alighted in a tall pine beside a humble, thatch-roofed cottage and sat gazing at the three travelers. Dathan glanced down at the book and saw that it was ablaze with intense white light. "This is the place," he told his companions. "The dove and the book both led us here."

He turned to his sister. "How's your hand?"

"It's still hurts," she said quietly, "but not nearly as much as it did."

Taking Lanna's good hand, Dathan turned toward the little cottage, but Sterling held him back. "Wait a moment," he urged in a quiet voice. "Let's look the place over. It would be good to know what we are getting ourselves into here."

The trio crept closer and then crouched for a moment in the undergrowth on the slope above the humble dwelling, silently watching the drama unfolding below them. Two knights were engaged in a desperate battle while a small crowd of spectators eagerly awaited the outcome. Swords clashed. The taller of the knights, a bareheaded man in his early thirties, was retreating before a furious attack by a much shorter knight. The smaller knight was relentless in his assault on the taller man, unleashing a withering volley of slices and thrusts with a ferocity that would have intimidated the most experienced of swordsmen.

The small crowd of spectators was clearly on the side of the smaller combatant, though he seemed determined to take off the head of the bigger man. They cheered each time the taller man retreated and groaned when he advanced. The short knight was an obvious favorite.

"Take that, sire!" the short knight cried, swinging his sword with both hands in a deadly cut intended to take off his opponent's head. "And that! And that!" The taller man struggled to defend himself, desperately parrying each blow from the relentless sword.

Dathan turned to Sterling. "How would you like to go against an opponent with that much vigor?"

Sterling laughed. "He battles with the heart of a lion, doesn't he?"

Just then the taller of the knights dropped to one knee and his held his sword aloft in a gesture of surrender. "I yield!" he cried in exhaustion. "I beg for mercy!"

With a huge grin of triumph on his youthful face, the victor, a little boy about four years of age, stepped forward and took the wooden sword from the taller knight. "Papa, did I win?"

"Aye, Silas, you won!" the father said, grabbing the youngster and embracing him. "You plain wore me out, son. I wish I had half the energy that you have."

"Excellent swordplay, Silas!" The spectators, two girls and a boy, gathered around the beaming boy to congratulate him. "You'll make quite a knight one day."

Sterling, Dathan, and Lanna strode down the hill toward the cottage. As they approached the house, the children spotted them and paused to regard them with interest coupled with suspicion. "Papa, someone's coming," little Silas announced.

The tall man turned, and as he spotted the three visitors, a worried look spread across his features. "Is there something I can do for you, my lord?" he asked, addressing Sterling.

"Sir," Sterling said, "we are on a quest for King Emmanuel and are just passing through. My friend Lanna burned her hand rather badly and we were hoping that you can help her."

A look of relief crossed the man's face as he studied Sterling. "You're Judan, aren't you?"

"Aye, sir." Sterling was taken aback by the man's bluntness.

A friendly smile suddenly brightened the man's countenance. "Come in! Come in!" he cried warmly, as his suspicions evaporated. "You are welcome here. I am Wallace. My wife will make a poultice for the burn and have your friend as good as new in no time."

Wallace leaned down, seized his small son by the hips, and flipped him head over heels to land sitting on his shoulder.

The boy laughed with delight. "Actually," the playful man said, "it's probably a good thing you came when you did. This little swordsman was wearing me out! I'm not sure how much more I could have taken."

The three visitors laughed at his words, abruptly feeling relaxed and right at home without even realizing it. "I'm Sterling," the Judan youth said, "and this is my friend Dathan and his sister, Lanna."

Wallace extended his hand in greeting to each of them. "Aye, it's good to have you here. You already met Silas. The other youngsters are Meri—she's the oldest girl—and Lissie and my other son Thane. Now, come inside so my wife can take a look at that hand."

Silas wiggled to get down from his father's shoulder. "Put me down, Papa! Please?"

The tall man lifted his young son down from his shoulder. Silas immediately extended his hand to Lanna. "Welcome to our abode, fair lady!" Laughter filled the yard.

Meri looked at her father. "Where did he learn that?"

Wallace shrugged and gave his son a puzzled glance as he led his visitors inside the little house. "Rosie!" he called, "we have guests."

A thin, tired-looking woman stepped into the room, wiping her hands on a tattered apron. She brightened when she saw the trio and hurried forward to meet them. "Welcome."

"My love, our friend Lanna has burned her hand," Wallace told his wife. "Would you help her care for the burn?"

"Certainly," the woman replied sweetly, beckoning to Lanna. "Come with me, dear; I have just the thing. We'll make a poultice of myrrh and aloes."

As the gentle peasant woman mixed a paste, her son Silas sat beside Lanna and stroked her arm as if to comfort her.

"Does it hurt bad?" he asked, looking up into her face with an expression of concern.

"It hurts quite a bit," she told him truthfully, "but not as much as it did before."

"How did you hurt it?" The gentle stroking increased in tempo.

"I fell into a fire and burned it."

Silas grimaced and closed his eyes for a moment as if he couldn't bear the thought. "I'm glad that you didn't get all burned up," he said, opening his eyes and staring intently at her.

Rosie began to wrap the aloe mixture in a primitive bandage around Lanna's injured hand. "Don't bother her, son," she scolded gently. "Perhaps Lanna doesn't feel like talking right now."

"Oh, that's all right," Lanna assured her. "You have a very caring little boy here. I like that."

"Caring?" his older brother Thane echoed. "You wouldn't have thought that when he was sword fighting Papa." Laughter filled the room.

"Silas is going to be quite a knight, Mama," Wallace told his wife. "I'm afraid he beat me at swordplay again this evening."

"Did he now, Papa?" Rosie replied, looking up from her work and giving Thane a broad wink. "So he's going to take your place as the best swordsman in the family, sire?"

"It's beginning to look that way," Wallace replied.

Dathan looked around the humble dwelling. The entire family was clustered closely around and it was very obvious that the members of this poor peasant family loved each other. The gentle way they spoke to each other, they way they touched each other, the look of admiration that Dathan saw in their eyes when they looked at their father—all the evidence told him that this was one happy family.

"There," Rosie said, as she tied a knot on the crude bandage, "that's the best I can do. Once the salve starts to work,

I think it will feel quite a bit better. And I do think that it will heal quite nicely. You can be thankful that the burn was not more serious."

"Thank you, ma'am," Lanna said quietly.

At that moment, the staccato of hoof beats broke upon the silence and Wallace leaped to his feet in alarm. He ran to the window and took a quick look. "Karnivans! There are at least a dozen of them!"

Dathan felt a cold stab of fear through his heart. If the Karnivan knights surrounded the house, there would be no escape. Sterling would be taken captive, and he and Lanna would be killed.

Dathan heard the sound of the horses as they swept into the yard and the shouted commands of a Karnivan officer. "Surround the house! Search the premises!"

"Quickly," Wallace urged the terror-stricken fugitives, "follow me!"

As if by a prearranged signal, Rosie and the children rushed to the front door.

Wallace darted into the back room with Lanna, Dathan, and Sterling right on his heels. The tall peasant seized the side of the doorframe and pulled it sharply to one side, then pulled it toward himself. To the astonishment of his three visitors, a section of the daub-and-wattle wall swung toward them, revealing a crude ladder embedded in the outer wall. "Climb quickly!" Wallace ordered. "When you reach the alcove, lie still. The Karnivans will never find you."

Sterling darted up the ladder and disappeared into a narrow space in the thatched ceiling. Lanna went right up behind him. Dathan followed and found them sliding into a narrow space between the rafters of the roof. As he crawled in, the wall swung shut and suddenly all was dark.

There's a double roof, Dathan realized, *with a hollow space between the two layers. What a perfect hiding place! When the wall closes, even the ladder is hidden!* As his eyes grew accustomed to the dim light, he could see that he and his trembling companions were lying on a lattice work of thin boards. His heart pounded as he discovered a gap in the thatching that allowed him to see into the room below.

At that moment, three Karnivan soldiers rushed into the room, thrusting the hapless Wallace before them. He sat down weakly on a stool. The peasant's children filed into the room and stood fearfully against the movable wall. Terrified, Dathan watched through the gap in the thatching.

"We're looking for three Judan youth," the leader of the soldiers snarled. He was a big man, powerfully built, with a handsome face. But his features were twisted with rage and hatred, and he reminded Dathan of a baligarb from a nightmare.

"Where are they?" the Karnivan captain demanded, shaking Wallace roughly by the shoulder.

Wallace shrugged, his lips compressed in a thin line. He wasn't telling. In the alcove, Dathan gasped, realizing what was about to happen to the kind, fun-loving father of four lively children. And it was all on their account. They had brought the Karnivan menace upon this innocent family. He debated calling out to save the poor peasant, but remembered that the lives of Lanna and Sterling were also at stake.

"You'll talk, you will!" The burly soldier raised his fist to strike Wallace. And then, his gaze fell upon Silas.

He lowered his hand. "Come here, little boy," he coaxed, his voice suddenly smooth and gentle. "I want to talk to you."

Silas' mother's eyes flashed angrily, but she said nothing. Silas walked obediently over to the soldier, who squatted beside him. To everyone's amazement, the little boy climbed upon the man's knee and put a tiny arm around his thick neck.

"I need to know something," the Karnivan captain said quietly. "And you'll tell me, won't you?"

Silas nodded in agreement. "Aye, Sir Knight."

"Were there three young people in the house?" Dathan saw Rosie stiffen slightly at the question. He glanced back to Silas, and, to his horror, saw him nod again! They were about to be discovered! "Are they here now?" Again, the curly little head nodded.

"Will you show me where they are?" the big Karnivan asked softly.

"Aye, Sir Knight." The little boy climbed down from the man's knee and marched triumphantly toward the movable section of wall!

Chapter Fifteen

Panic-stricken, Dathan held his breath as Silas walked toward the wall with a happy smile on his angelic little face. Fear gripped him. He, Lanna, and Sterling were about to be betrayed to the merciless Karnivans by the innocent enthusiasm of a four-year-old!

Silas' mother, Rosie, watched her little son in horror. Her eyes pleaded with Silas to stop, but she dared not say anything. The rest of the family stood quietly awaiting the inevitable.

At that moment the front door burst open and two Karnivan knights hurried into the room. "Sire," one said, addressing the Karnivan captain, "the three fugitives have been spotted less than a mile from here, heading south. Our informant saw three young travelers that match their description perfectly. If we make haste we can overtake them."

The captain hesitated for an instant and then turned toward the door. "Let's ride." Without a backward glance, the Karnivans rushed from the room. Seconds later, the welcome sound of horses' hooves announced their departure.

Wallace held up one hand as a signal for his family to remain still. Five minutes passed. Finally, he stood to his feet and slipped quietly out the back door. He returned in a few moments, carefully bolting the front and back doors as he came in. "The Karnivans are gone," he said softly, and Silas cheered. "We have to be quiet," the man warned. "They may still be close by."

He opened the movable wall, brightening the alcove with the additional light. "I think it's safe to come down now," he said quietly. "The Karnivans seem to have left the area."

Lanna, Dathan, and Sterling climbed down from their hiding place in the narrow alcove and Wallace closed the wall behind them. "That was scary!" Lanna remarked, and Dathan saw that she was still trembling.

He slipped over beside her and embraced her. "That was too close," he agreed. "I thought for sure we were going to be captured!"

"Praise be to Emmanuel that you were not discovered," Wallace said fervently.

Sterling was examining the movable wall. "This is ingenious," he declared, running his hands along the doorframe as if to find the locking mechanism. "To all appearances this is an ordinary wall. One would never guess that it moves, or that it conceals the entrance to a secret chamber." He glanced upward at the thatched roof. "And the hiding place itself is equally ingenious! Who would guess that the roof is thick enough to hide in?"

He turned to Wallace with a puzzled expression. "Who designed this? And why?"

The peasant smiled. "My family and I are part of an... an alliance, shall we say, that came together for the purpose of helping the Judan people escape the terrors of Grimlor and the Karnivans. We assist Judan travelers in their flight from Karniva to Ainranon and other countries that are safe havens. The secret chamber was constructed for that very purpose, and as you saw tonight, it works. The Karnivans have searched our home several times, but as yet have no idea that the chamber is there."

Sterling was impressed. "That's incredible! You actually built the alcove to help the Judan people escape the Karnivans?"

"Aye," Wallace replied. "Many have taken refuge here for a night or two on their journey to Ainranon." He grimaced. "On two occasions we have had, uh, shall we say, close calls, just as we had tonight."

The Judan youth was still incredulous. "But sir," he said, "by helping my people, are you not putting your family in danger?"

"We are all in danger as long as Grimlor and the Karnivans rule Karniva," Wallace answered soberly. "Aye, there is a threat of danger in what we are doing. But the Judans are King Emmanuel's own people, sire, and we trust in his protection as we attempt to assist his people."

A somber expression crossed Sterling's face. "I am grateful for what you are doing, sir. May King Emmanuel's protection always be upon you and your family."

Wallace glanced at his wife. "I do not think that it would be safe for you to remain here tonight. The Karnivans may return at any moment, and if they catch us by surprise, you could be taken captive." When he saw the looks of dismay that appeared on the faces of the fugitives, he held up both hands. "Wait—we are not throwing you out in the cold. We have another option. There is a cave not far from here that is safer and more secluded than the alcove. For the moment, you need to hide in the fields behind the house. As soon as it is dark, I will lead you to the cave."

Dathan spoke up. "We are grateful, sir, for your help. As Sterling mentioned, you and your family have risked much for us, and we thank you."

Four shadows moved like phantoms as they silently trekked up a steep ridge. The half moon hung low in the heavens, partially obscured from time to time by wispy clouds that insisted on passing across its face. An owl hooted in the distance as if to dispel its own loneliness. The night was young and the creatures of the night were just beginning to stir.

"The cave is just beyond this next rise," Wallace told his charges as they hiked through the darkness. "It is so well concealed that you could pass within five paces of the opening and never see it. Very few people know of its existence." He smiled. "Except for Judan travelers, of course."

Moments later, as they topped the rise, the tall peasant abruptly stopped, his body rigid. Sterling leaned close. "What is it?" he whispered.

"Stand perfectly still," Wallace whispered. "Make no noise. This doesn't look good." For several long moments he scanned the darkness, moving only his eyes. "I fear that our hiding place has been discovered," he whispered. "Someone has built a signal fire less than ten paces from the cave's mouth. The fire has gone out, but the coals remain." He pointed. "There. See the glowing coals? The entrance to the cave is just beyond that."

Sterling began to laugh, and Wallace rebuked him. "I don't think you realize how serious this is, my young friend. Countless numbers of your own people have spent the night in safety in this cave on their way to freedom in Ainranon. We have a route of safe homes and castles stretching across Karniva from north to south; a chain, as it were. But if one link is compromised, as it seems that this haven is, then the entire chain is jeopardized. Can you not see that?" Dathan was surprised at how indignant the soft-spoken peasant had become.

But Sterling continued to laugh. "There is nothing to fear," he told Wallace. "Your secret hiding place has not been discovered or jeopardized."

"How can you say that, Sterling?" Dathan challenged, becoming a bit irked by his friend's attitude. "If someone has built a fire here, then perhaps the cave has been discovered."

"I know the night is dark," Sterling replied, "but don't you see where we are? We are the ones who built the fire! This is where Lanna burned herself!"

Wallace turned to face him in the moonlight. "Are you certain, son? Dead certain?"

"I'm positive, sir. We stopped here late in the afternoon and made preparations to spend the night. We were the ones who built the fire and then abandoned it when we sought help for Lanna's burn."

Wallace let out his breath in a long sigh. "You can't imagine how relieved I am to hear that."

"You are right about one thing, sir," Sterling replied.

"And what is that?"

"Apparently, your cave is well hidden. We prepared to camp here and never saw it."

The peasant made a torch from a dead branch and lit it from the hot coals. "We need to erase all signs of this fire," he told the fugitives, "for it could lead the enemy to this place." While Lanna held the torch, Wallace, Sterling, and Dathan carried handfuls of water from the stream, completely dousing the fire. They then scattered the ashes far and wide and obliterated all traces of the fire.

Wallace took the torch and led them to a tangle of elderberry bushes against the rocky face of the hillside less than ten paces from the site of their fire. He handed the flickering torch to Sterling and then parted the bushes to reveal a small opening in the rocky face. "You go first, Sterling. Once inside, you'll find a cruse of water, food supplies, and sleeping pallets."

He scanned the area to make certain that they were not being observed and then continued. "Your next stop on the journey will be at an abandoned castle, the Castle of Consecration. Two brothers live there, and they will provide for your needs and then give you directions to the next location. Here's how to find the castle..."

After giving them directions, Wallace embraced each of the fugitives. "Travel in safety, my young friends, and may the love of King Emmanuel protect and keep you." With these words, he disappeared into the darkness of the night.

"The castle of which Wallace spoke is just ahead," Sterling told the twins, as he studied the parchment in his hand. "According to the map, it should be at the head of this valley."

The three fugitives had traveled hard that day, trekking long distances with very brief rest periods, for Wallace had told them that the Castle of Consecration was quite a distance away. He had been right. The afternoon shadows were growing long and the sun was thinking of retiring for the night as they exited a narrow valley and saw the ruins of a castle on a promontory less than a mile away.

"The Castle of Consecration," Dathan said quietly, as he surveyed the ruined structure. "Wallace said that at one time it was a magnificent castle, one of the grandest in all Terrestria."

"I wonder what happened to it," said Lanna.

"If it was a castle belonging to King Emmanuel, and I'm sure it must have been, perhaps it was attacked by Argamor's dark forces."

"Let's hurry," Sterling urged. "We have barely an hour of daylight left." As the trio hiked toward the castle Sterling told his companions, "You know, I had that crazy dream again last night."

"The one about fishing in the moat at Windstone Castle?" Dathan asked.

Sterling nodded. "I've had the same dream several times now. I wonder what it means. Each time, I'm a little boy, and I'm with a big, big man. I think he had blond hair."

"Lord Keidric," Lanna suggested with a grin.

Sterling snorted. "Right." He frowned. "The dream is beginning to bother me. I can't help but wonder if it has some significance."

A short while later they approached the ruins. "The closer you get, the more disheartening it is to view it," Dathan said quietly.

Just ahead, partially hidden in a tangle of weeds and brambles, stood the ruins of the large concentric castle. Rotting timbers and beams leaned against crumbling walls and towers. Shattered blocks of limestone littered the ground. A slight depression in the earth marked the location of the moat, but it had long ago been filled in with dirt and debris. Crumbling fragments of wood and some rusty hardware were all that remained of the massive drawbridge.

As the travelers stepped closer to the decaying wall and approached the opening that had once been the main gate, a raucous screech from just above their heads caused them to jump with fright. They looked up to see a pair of huge ravens atop the ruined wall, opening and closing their beaks as they watched the intruders with beady eyes. "This castle, once so elegant and proud," Dathan said aloud, and his voice echoed strangely, "is now the home of dirty scavenger birds."

Lanna drew back. "Let's not go in."

"This is our home for the night," her brother replied. "Wallace told us that it's safe."

Sterling heard a slight noise and turned just in time to catch a glimpse of a red fox darting through a hole in the wall. Intrigued, he decided to follow it. Ducking through the breach in the wall, he pushed through a tangle of briars and entered the castle ruins. He found himself in the barbican, the narrow courtyard between the outer and inner walls of the castle. The barbican was choked with weeds. Beneath a gnarled and twisted eucalyptus tree, he saw the crumbled remains of a once elegant stone bench. Passing through a breach in the inner wall, he entered the bailey, or inner courtyard.

Still outside the castle, the twins hesitantly passed through the openings that had once been the main gate and the inner gate and then paused to survey the ruined bailey. The courtyard lay before them, a scene of neglect and decay. An enormous statue of a knight, once magnificent but now shattered and disfigured, occupied a place of prominence. The bailey was cluttered with boulders and debris; piles of marble and mortar lay scattered about. A squirrel darted across the rubble and leaped into the branches of a twisted, stunted oak. Dathan felt a pang of remorse as he studied the now silent ruins. "This castle, once so beautiful," he sighed aloud, "now the habitation of ravens and squirrels. Such a shame! I wonder what happened."

Strange, unexplainable sensations swept over him. Recognition. Shadowed memories. An indescribable sense of loss, as though a friend had just died. *This castle looks nothing like Windstone Castle,* he realized, *and yet, there's something familiar about this and I almost feel that I have been here before.* He scanned the crumbling walls. *I wonder when it was built, and how long it has been abandoned.*

As Dathan stepped carefully over a pile of debris, the sunlight glinted on a half-buried object, catching his attention. He stooped and tried to pull the object free, but it wouldn't move. After kicking some of the dirt away with the toe of his shoe, he was able to pull it free. He stared.

"What did you find?" Lanna asked.

"It's a knight's shield, badly dented," her brother replied slowly, transfixed as though he couldn't take his eyes from it. "I wonder..."

Placing the shield face down in the grass and weeds, he rubbed it vigorously back and forth to knock off some of the dirt. He was stunned when he turned the shield back over. The coat of arms was that of King Emmanuel.

Sterling approached at that moment. "This place is eerie," he said in a quiet voice, almost as if he were afraid of disturbing the solitude of the ruins. "You can almost feel the presence of the knights who once defended this castle. It's as if we're being watched."

"I feel the same thing," Dathan replied, glancing uneasily around the ruins.

"Stand where you are!" a gruff voice suddenly ordered. "Don't move, as you value your life!"

The three fugitives froze.

"Relax, Vaden," a second voice admonished, "it's just three youth. I'm sure they mean no harm."

"They're Karnivans, as I live and breathe," the gruff voice responded. "We'd do well to drop them with arrows here and now."

"Come now, Vaden, they're not Karnivans."

"Of course they are! Look at the girl. Did you ever see such yellow hair? They're Karnivans, I tell you; Karnivan spies."

"I really doubt that."

"I say we drop them before they have a chance to do their dastardly deeds. An arrow through the heart for each of them." The gruff voice was harsh and grating, like the sound of a wooden boat being dragged across a gravel bar, and the owner sounded as if he was serious about his intentions. Dathan held his breath, hoping desperately that his companion would talk him out of trying.

"Look at the tall one, Vaden. That's a Judan lad if I ever saw one." The second voice was pleasant, almost melodious, like the warble of a meadowlark.

"Well, I declare," the gruff voice exclaimed. "I do believe you're right, Dane." There was a long moment's silence, and then, "Turn around slowly. Make any wrong moves and my brother and I will put arrows through your hearts."

Slowly, fearfully, the three fugitives turned around and were astounded to find that the bailey entrance was empty. There was no one there. Dathan felt a surge of fear. *Are spirits guarding this old castle?* He wanted desperately to draw his sword, but refrained from doing so. *How can you fight an enemy you cannot see?*

"See! What did tell you, Vaden? It's a young lass and two young squires. If those are Karnivans then I'm the king of Karniva."

The voices came from somewhere above the three fugitives. Dathan looked up to see two brawny archers on the sentrywalk above the bailey. At the moment, both men had their longbows pulled to full draw, and the weapons were pointed at Dathan and his companions. "Please don't shoot!" Lanna cried out. "We are not Karnivans."

One of the archers immediately relaxed his bow and lowered the arrow, but his companion glared at them and continued to hold them at bowpoint. "How do we know that you're not Karnivans?"

"Wallace sent us," Sterling blurted. "He told us you would shelter us for the night. We're on our way to Ainranon."

"Wallace!" The gruff-voiced archer lowered his weapon. "Well, why didn't you say so?"

"We'll be right down," his companion said, and both men hurried across the sentrywalk to the flight of stairs that led down into the bailey. The trio watched as they approached. Both men were of medium height, but their large hands, thick arms, and massive shoulders told of tremendous strength. They were clad in rusty coats of mail and wore battered helmets that had seen better days, but both wore swords and carried longbows. Their beards of gray and the stiffness with which they walked testified to their advancing age.

"I'm Dane," one archer said as he extended his hand in greeting, and his voice was smooth. "My gravel-voiced brother is the one who wished to kill you. His name is Vaden."

"One can't be too careful," Vaden muttered, as if to excuse the suspicious welcome he had proffered. He extended his hand to each of them in turn. "You are welcome at the Castle of Consecration and we are glad to have you. I am sorry if my reception was a bit severe at first."

Sterling smiled to set the man at ease. "As you said, one can never be too careful."

"Vaden and I were just about to conclude our watch and go to supper when we saw your approach," Dane told them. "Would you do us the honor of joining us for a meal?"

"The honor would be ours," Sterling replied.

"Then why not meet us in the great hall," Dane suggested, "just as soon as Vaden and I finish our watch."

"Even with the castle in ruins, you still stand watch?" Dathan was incredulous.

"Every day," Vaden grated, "for the last thirty-three years.

We'll be faithful to our post until King Emmanuel comes or relieves us of duty." He glanced at the setting sun as he headed for the stairs. "Come, Brother, for we still have six minutes on watch."

Sterling and his companions made their way toward the roofless great hall. "Unusual men, aren't they?" Sterling commented. "Imagine serving sentry duty in a castle such as this."

"For thirty-three years," Dathan interjected.

"Are they really brothers?" Lanna asked.

"Dane said that they were and he seemed to be telling the truth," Dathan replied. "He doesn't seem like the type of man who would jest."

"Karnivans approaching the castle!" Vaden's gravelly voice echoed and re-echoed within the empty confines of the bailey. Startled, the trio looked up at the sentrywalk to see the two brothers gesturing wildly.

"Quick!" Dane shouted. "Up the stairs and into the north tower! There's a band of knights approaching the castle and they can be none other than the Karnivans! We'll try to hold them off!" As he spoke, he and Vaden began unleashing a volley of arrows over the outer curtain wall.

"Run for it!" Sterling urged, and took off like a fox pursued by hounds. The twins were right behind him.

The fugitives reached the door of the north tower at the same moment as the two sentries. Flinging open the door, Vaden bellowed, "Up the stairs, my young friends!" A score of Karnivan knights swarmed into the bailey, spotted their quarry, and started for the tower with cries of triumph. The trio lost no time scrambling up the spiraling stairs to the top of the tower.

Moments later, as the last of the little group burst onto the battlements of the tower, Dane dropped the massive trap door and then knelt and secured it with four heavy bolts. “Nine inches thick,” he told them, as he rose to his feet. “They’ll never batter their way through that.”

“Can’t they burn us out?” Sterling inquired.

“They can and they will,” the old man replied. “It will take a few hours, but if they start immediately, we’ll all be dead about the time the sun comes up tomorrow.”

Chapter Sixteen

Dathan's heart was racing as he leaned over the tower battlements and looked at the angry band of Karnivans thirty-two feet below. Dark eyes glittered with hatred as they saw him and snarls of rage assaulted him. The Karnivans were a pack of savage animals, thirsty for blood and anxious for the kill. He swallowed hard and his breath came in trembling gasps.

Lanna gripped his hand. "What are we going to do?"

Dathan shook his head. "I-I don't know." He looked at Sterling, but the Judan youth was as terrified as he.

"Send a petition," a quiet voice said, and the group turned as one to see the beautiful dove perched on a merlon and regarding them with unblinking eyes. There was a certain calmness, a peace, about him, and his presence quieted their troubled hearts.

"Did you speak?" Lanna asked, with trembling lips.

"Send a petition," the dove repeated. "You have that right as the children of His Majesty."

Dathan had his book out in a moment and eagerly snatched the parchment from within its pages. Kneeling, he spread the petition upon his thigh and then realized that he had no writing instrument. To his great astonishment, Dane handed him a quill and a bottle of ink. The trembling boy hastily penned the following message:

"To His Majesty, King Emmanuel:

We are trapped in a tower of the Castle of Consecration and the situation seems hopeless. Please, Your Majesty, send help immediately.

Your son, Dathan."

Rolling the parchment up, he released it and watched as the petition shot from his hand and soared over the horizon in a moment's time. Just then there was a heavy thud from the wooden door at the base of the tower and a loud grunt. "There will be no escape," a rough voice called from down below, "so you might as well give yourselves up! If we have to burn you out it will go all the worse with you. Why not make it easy on yourselves and us? Lord Grimlor will have you either way."

Will King Emmanuel answer us? Dathan wondered in desperation. *Will he send someone to our aid? Will Lanna, Sterling, and I die here in the tower, or will the King provide a way of escape?*

"You have the mighty sword of King Emmanuel," said the quiet voice of the dove. Dathan turned and stared at the snowy white bird.

He turned to Dane. "What if we were to battle our way out of this?" he asked, swallowing hard as he said the words, for the very idea struck terror into his heart.

The old sentry shook his head. "There are a score of them, lad. There are only four of us."

"Five," Lanna corrected.

"Even so, five swords are no match for a score of Karnivan swords," Dane answered mournfully. "And to be honest, Vaden and I are too old to fight. Nay, lad, if we tried to fight our way out, we'd be slaughtered within moments."

"We have His Majesty's sword," Dathan replied quietly, and a charge of hope surged through his being as he said the words. "They have only the weapons of the flesh." He drew his sword and turned to Sterling. "Will you go with me against the Karnivans? We will go in the name of King Emmanuel and in the power of his might. Though there be a score of the enemy, the victory is ours if we trust in our King."

The Judan youth drew his sword. "I will go."

"And I," said Lanna, drawing her sword.

Dathan looked at Dane and Vaden. "Gentlemen?"

Both men looked uncomfortable. "We have not used the sword of Emmanuel in recent years," they replied. "We are more skilled in the use of the longbow."

"Then stay in the tower and use your bows to turn the battle in our favor," Sterling told them, and Dathan thought he detected a note of disdain in his voice, "but my companions and I will go against the enemy face to face."

"May Emmanuel's protection be upon you," Dane replied quietly, "though the odds are definitely not in your favor."

"Ready?" Sterling asked Dathan and Lanna. "Once we unbar the lower door, let's fly upon the enemy with speed and force. Perhaps we can take them by surprise."

"Lanna, stay right behind us and watch our backs," Dathan told his sister. "And remember, we battle in the name and power of King Emmanuel."

With their hearts in their throats they descended the spiraling stair and then paused at the door. "Well, this is it," Sterling said quietly. "If we die in this battle, I want you to know that I am grateful to you both for accompanying me on this quest."

"Our hope is in the name of Emmanuel and the power of his sword," Dathan replied quietly. "Our lives are in his hands."

Sterling raised his sword. "Ready?" He and Dathan lifted the bars and threw the door wide open, startling the band of

Karnivan knights clustered at the base of the tower. "For the glory of King Emmanuel!" Dathan shouted, as he, Sterling, and Lanna exploded through the doorway with swords striking like lightning. The suddenness of their attack caught the enemy off guard, and two Karnivans fell dead before they had time to draw their swords.

The trio abruptly found themselves surrounded by a ring of snarling Karnivans with menacing swords. Leaping forward fearlessly, they engaged the enemy and the bailey rang with the sounds of the battle. Dathan's heart constricted with fear as two enormous knights bore down upon him with snarls of rage. Their swords were swift, and for a moment, Dathan struggled to defend himself against the assault, for he had already forgotten where his strength lay and battled in his own strength. A broadsword came slashing down fiercely and he barely raised his sword in time to deflect the blow. "Emmanuel, help us!" he cried.

His adversary grunted and dropped his sword as an arrow suddenly embedded itself in his arm. Dathan leaped forward and with one swing of the mighty sword ended his life. His companion looked skyward for the briefest instant, and Dathan seized the opportunity to inflict a mortal wound. The man retreated.

"Dathan, help me!" Lanna cried, and Dathan spun around to see his sister retreating before the slashing sword of a tall Karnivan. The knight was relentless, cutting and thrusting furiously, and the girl was hard pressed to defend herself. Dathan leaped to her rescue, but before he could bring his sword into play, an arrow struck the man in the shoulder. Gripping his sword, he grunted as he attempted to raise it, but it was too late. Lanna's sword ended his life.

Darkness stole over the Castle of Consecration as the battle raged. Though hopelessly outnumbered, the three young fugitives fought with the courage of lions, knowing that their lives and perhaps the future of Cheswold were at stake. Wielding the mighty swords fashioned by King Emmanuel himself and aided by a barrage of arrows from the two elderly archers in the tower, they at last prevailed.

"Only four Karnivans left," Sterling grunted wearily, as he, Dathan, and Lanna stood back to back in the center of the bailey, trying desperately to catch their breath and waiting as the enemy knights regrouped. "The battle is ours."

"Not yet," Dathan admonished. "And remember, we battle only in His Majesty's might."

Screaming with rage, the four remaining Karnivans exploded from the shadows and rushed across the bailey in a direct assault. A well-placed arrow struck one in the back of the thigh, dropping him to the cobblestones. Shoulder to shoulder, Sterling and the twins stood their ground and defended their position against the three powerful adversaries. Within moments, two Karnivan knights lay dead upon the ground and the lone adversary turned to flee. An arrow from the tower cut him down before he took three steps.

"Praise to King Emmanuel!" Dathan cried, lifting his sword in the moonlight. "The victory is ours!"

"The victory is his," Lanna reminded softly.

"You're less than a day's travel from the border of Ainranon," Dane told the trio as he and Vaden served them breakfast the next morning. "But beware, for it is at the border that you will find your greatest danger. Our reports tell us that the Karnivans have closed the border."

"It's hard to believe that we are this close to Ainranon," Lanna said happily.

Dane gave her a hard look. "You are not there yet. This is no time to relax your guard, for you do not yet know what you are facing."

When the simple meal was finished, the two brothers accompanied them to the castle entrance. Vaden handed Dathan a package. "Vittles for today," he said simply.

"We are grateful for your assistance," Sterling told the men. "You have helped us greatly and we are in your debt."

"May His Majesty smile upon you as you finish your journey," Dane replied. "It has been an honor to have you here at the castle."

"I still can't believe that we're this close," Lanna gushed later that morning. "We've been traveling and traveling and it sometimes seemed that we would never reach Ainranon. But we're almost there!"

She glanced at Dathan and saw a glum look on his face. "Well, aren't you excited? Our quest is almost over!"

He shrugged "Maybe."

"But Dathan, think of all we've been through! It's over! We're almost there! Once we reach Ainranon, we can rest easy and know that we accomplished our mission."

"Once we reach Ainranon, we have nowhere to go," her brother replied.

"What?" She stared at him.

"Lanna, don't you realize that we have no home? We have nowhere to go! We have no family—no one cares if we live or die. And we certainly can't go back to Windstone Castle; Lord Keidric would kill us as runaway slaves."

A look of concern appeared on Lanna's face. "I never thought about that," she said slowly.

"Well, I have," her brother retorted. "Once we cross the border into Ainranon and Sterling reaches Lord Stratford safely, we have no purpose in life. We have nowhere to go. Lanna, I really don't know what we're going to do. Sure, I'm anxious to get to Ainranon and know that we are safe and that we have fulfilled our quest, but in some ways I'm not really looking forward to it. I don't have any idea what we are going to do or where we are going to live."

"I wish we knew where Papa is," Lanna sighed wistfully. "Dathan, I miss him so! Especially now."

"I know, I know," Dathan replied. "I miss him every day of my life."

"What if we could go back to Cheswold, back to our shire? What if we could find Papa and live with him again? Oh, Dathan..."

"We'd never make it back alive," her brother said with a sigh. "And I wouldn't know how to find Papa. When the creditor took Papa's shop and sold us, Papa had to move to another region. Finding him would be like trying to find a pebble in a pond."

"But couldn't we try, Dathan?"

Dathan sighed heavily. "Oh, Lanna, I don't know what to do..."

They talked about the problem from time to time throughout the rest of the day. Sterling tried to encourage them and even offer advice, but the problem was theirs and he knew that they would have to find their own solution.

Dark clouds were rolling in from the west as they made their way through a grassy valley late that afternoon. The wind gusted and howled, swirling the grasses in rolling patterns that looked like waves of the sea and spitefully throwing dust and debris in their faces as if it resented their trespassing. Occasional drops of rain spattered down, giving threats of an imminent downpour, but the storm was somehow delayed. The skies took on an ominous, greenish-gray hue.

"I don't like the looks of this weather," Sterling shouted above the din of the wind. "I think we're in for one really bad storm."

"The sky looks frightening," Lanna shouted back. "It looks like something really bad is going to happen."

As they reached the head of the valley, they found that it divided into two, with the vale to the left wide and inviting, while the vale to the right was narrow and dark. "Which way do we go?" Dathan wondered aloud.

Sterling crouched in the lee of a rocky outcropping and spread his map upon his knee. "According to this we take the path to the left," he reported. "That would take us to the southeast and toward Ainranon." He glanced at the trail ahead. "The path to the left is more pleasant anyway. The one to the right looks dangerous, like a place the Karnivans could plan an ambush."

Dathan opened his book. "According to the book, we're to take the trail to the right."

Sterling snorted. "Go that way if you wish, my friend, but I'm going to the left."

Dathan stared at him. "You would ignore the guidance of the book?"

The Judan youth shrugged. "I'm just following the guidance of the map. It says to go to the left, and that makes more sense anyway, since that would lead us on a more direct route to Ainranon."

Lanna opened her book, studied it for a moment, and then sided with her brother. "My book also says to go to the right."

"So follow the path you want," Sterling retorted. "I'm taking the path that leads to Ainranon."

"Check your book," Lanna challenged. "See what it says."

"Oh, all right!" Sterling fumed. "Anything to make you happy." He opened his book and turned it slowly from side to side. Neither twin had to ask him what it said; the look on his face gave them the answer. Without a word he closed the volume and stowed it within his doublet once again.

At that moment, the dove swept down from a tall pine, circled once overhead as if to draw their attention, and then flew directly into the narrow valley to the right. Dathan glanced at Sterling. "Now do you have any doubts?" Sterling shrugged and without a word turned toward the trail to the right.

The three fugitives had trekked another two or three furlongs when they began to notice their surroundings with a growing sense of dismay. The trail wound its way between tall spires and rocky outcroppings that looked like creatures from another world. The forest was dark and gloomy here; the trees were gnarled and twisted specimens that sagged and drooped over the narrow trail like crippled old men. Blotches of dark moss hung from their shriveled limbs like tattered clothing. The air was dank and chill and reeked of decay.

"I don't like this," Lanna moaned, looking about in fright. "This looks really bad..."

"Keep walking," Dathan urged in a low voice. "We're following the book."

The forest grew darker. Realizing that he had not seen the dove for some time, Dathan glanced around, but the snowy white form of the celestial guide was nowhere to be seen. The wind howled mournfully through the twisted trees, moaning one moment and screeching the next as if it resented the presence of the young travelers. Dathan shivered and drew his cloak more tightly about him. Fear grew within him. For just a moment he considered suggesting that they retrace their steps and leave the canyon, but he quickly put the thought behind him and pushed resolutely onward. They would make it. Were they not following the guidance of Emmanuel's book?

The trail became narrower. Brambles and briars clutched at their clothing as they passed. The trees seemed to reach for them, snatching at their arms and faces with withered, gnarled branches as if they were determined to hold them back. The travelers trembled as they stumbled along in the darkness and gloom.

Lanna stopped in the middle of the trail. Dathan could tell that she was close to tears. "What's wrong?" he whispered.

"Something's following us," she whimpered. "I can hear it in the bushes beside the trail."

"Keep walking," Sterling urged in a subdued voice. "I don't like the looks of this either, but something tells me it would be a mistake to go back."

Soon the trees of the forest gave way to stunted shrubs, twisted thorn bushes, and creeping vines. Clumps of sharp-bladed sawgrass and thorny briars appeared along the trail. Steaming mud pots on both sides of the trail bubbled and hissed, releasing little clouds of noxious vapors into the air. The travelers' eyes burned so fiercely that they could barely keep them open. The air had become bitter and foul, stinging their eyes and searing their throats. They struggled to breathe, rubbing their burning eyes as they stumbled along. Poisonous vapors swirled across the trail, making them dizzy, nauseous, and disoriented.

As the trio passed between two tall outcroppings of sandstone, dark figures sprang from each side of the trail, striking Sterling and Dathan and bearing them to the ground. Lanna screamed as strong hands grabbed her from behind and a muscular arm locked itself around her neck in an iron embrace from which there would be no escape. Suddenly the trail was filled with shouting men brandishing weapons.

The fugitives were quickly bound with their hands behind them and then lifted to their feet. They found themselves staring into the stern faces of the knights from Windstone Castle. Dathan groaned inwardly when he recognized their captors. Just miles from the safety of Ainranon, he and his companions had been captured by Sir Keidric's men!

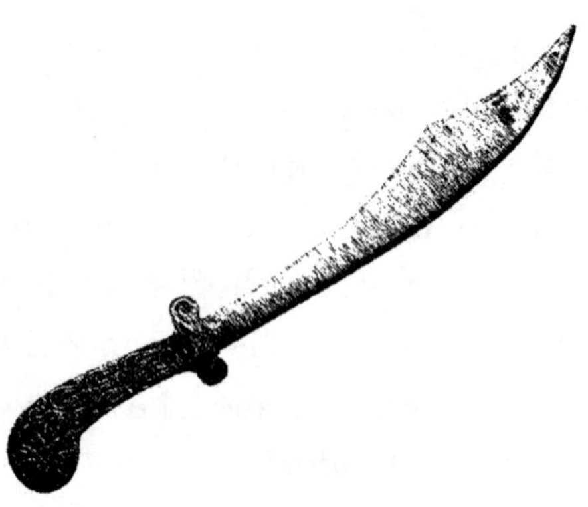

Chapter Seventeen

Terror swept over the fugitives as they recognized their captors. Falling into the hands of Sir Keidric was as fatal as being captured by the Karnivans. Dathan and Lanna faced certain death as runaway slaves, and Sterling would be delivered into the clutches of evil Grimlor. The quest for Ainranon had ended in failure.

"You insisted on following the book," Sterling said bitterly to Dathan and Lanna. "Look where it got us."

One of the knights grinned cheerfully at them. "Sorry to have to bind you," he said glibly, "but we're just following orders. Do you know how long we've been pursuing you?"

"Why don't you just run us through and be done with it?" Sterling snarled.

The knight gave him a strange look. "Surely you jest. Why would we do that?"

The captives were marched two or three furlongs down the narrow trail and then the company halted as they approached a tall man astride a powerful white stallion. Dathan's heart lurched. Sir Keidric, of Windstone Castle! Terrified, he found that he could not even look up at the man.

"Well, well, well," Sir Keidric said with a note of satisfaction in his voice as he dismounted. "What have we here? It seems that the hounds have finally brought the phantom foxes to bay. Do you three know what a difficult time we've had catching up with you?"

Lanna trembled as she asked, "What will you do with us, sire?"

"My men and I have pursued you halfway across Cheswold and all the way across Karniva," the tall nobleman told them with a shake of his head. "For a time it seemed that we were pursuing phantoms. No matter how hard we pushed, somehow you managed to stay one step ahead of us. We missed you by half a day here, two hours there." He laughed. "But that's behind us and we finally caught up with you."

He glanced at one of his men. "Please, untie them. Why were they bound?"

"Sire," one knight replied, "you ordered us to do whatever it took to make sure that they did not escape again."

Sir Keidric laughed. "Aye, but I didn't mean this."

Within moments, the three fugitives were free of their bonds. Dathan glanced around to see if an escape was possible, but the Windstone knights had surrounded them in a tight circle. There would be no escape.

Sterling stepped forward boldly. "Sire, you have me," he said, "so you accomplished your purpose. Do what you will with me, sire, but I beg you, show mercy to Lanna and Dathan."

The big man frowned. "What are you talking about?"

"I know the penalty for runaway slaves, sire, but please show mercy. My father is the Marquis of Marden. I give you my word; he will buy them from you at a good price. Please, sire."

Sir Keidric stood speechless for several seconds. He glanced at his men, looking from one to another as a thoughtful look crossed his face. Turning to Sterling and the twins, he studied their faces for a long moment. At last he spoke. "Do you have any idea," he asked slowly, "why my men and I have pursued you across two countries?"

"So you can kill Dathan and me as runaways and turn Sterling over to Grimlor and the Karnivans," Lanna blurted.

Sir Keidric looked at his men again. "No wonder they ran from us at the inn. They were under the impression..." He paused without finishing the sentence and then turned to face the three trembling fugitives. "My men and I have ridden halfway across Terrestria, or so it seems, for the sole purpose of saving you from the Karnivans! We are your allies, not your enemies!"

He began to laugh as he turned to his men again. "All these miles because of a simple misunderstanding!" Still laughing and shaking his head, he said to the bewildered trio, "Our purpose was not to capture you—our purpose was to save you!"

Sterling clenched his jaw. "We don't believe you."

The tall nobleman looked him in the eye. "Why not, lad?"

"We heard you outside the inn," the Judan youth replied fiercely, "telling your men to capture us and kill us!"

Sir Keidric opened his mouth to speak and then paused with a puzzled expression. "I told my men to capture and kill you?"

"Aye, sire. We couldn't hear everything you said, but we did hear that part."

Sir Keidric was distressed. "Lad, I never..."

"My lord, may I speak?" One of the knights stepped forward.

"Certainly, Sir Lionel."

"Sire, I do recall that you told us in the roadway in front of the inn that we must give diligence to find these young fugitives before the Karnivans could capture and kill them. Perhaps that is what this young lord overheard."

Sir Keidric looked at Sterling. "There you have it, lad. Does that answer your question?"

Sterling looked defiant. "Then why did your men imprison me in your dungeon?"

"I was not at Windstone that night," the nobleman replied. "I was on a quest..." He stopped in mid-sentence. "This is going to take some time in the telling. Why don't we go back to camp and enjoy supper together while I tell you the whole story and lay your fears to rest? If you know as little about this as you seem to, you're not ready for what I have to tell you." He grinned at them. "You three are in for the surprise of your life!"

His face abruptly took on a grave expression as he turned to Sterling. "I have to know one thing before another minute passes—do you have the dagger?"

Sterling hung his head. "The Karnivans have it, sire. They captured us, briefly, and they took it from us. I'm sorry, sire."

Sir Keidric expressed himself in a long sigh of resignation. "So am I, lad, so am I." He shrugged. "Well, I don't suppose that anything can be done about that now. Let's head for camp, shall we?"

"I'm sorry, sire," Sterling said again. "I suppose this means that our quest has ended in failure."

"Oh, not at all," Sir Keidric said mysteriously, "Not at all. There is more to this drama than you know."

The three fugitives followed Sir Keidric and his men through the woods, down a side trail and into a secluded war camp that nestled in a dark forest in a hidden valley. Dathan was amazed to see that hundreds of tents were hidden among the trees. Even more surprising was the reception that the nobleman received as the entourage passed through the camp. Each man that they passed stood and saluted, and their faces showed that Sir Keidric was held in high esteem. Knight and nobleman alike treated him as a superior.

Darkness stole over the camp as the Windstone knights and their leader led the three fugitives to a campfire that leaped and danced before the largest of the tents. A servant hurried forward to meet them. "I've been holding supper, sire. Are you and the men ready to eat?"

"Aye," Sir Keidric replied, "but we are to have three guests tonight."

"Very well, sire."

Within minutes, the Windstone entourage and the three fugitives were seated around the fire, enjoying a welcome meal of roast venison and pheasant, flat bread, and roast corn and apples. As they ate, Sterling removed his boot to get at the sheath, which had slid beneath his foot and was becoming quite uncomfortable. Drawing the grimy sheath from within his boot, he dropped it on the ground beside his foot and then replaced his boot.

Sir Keidric noticed. "What is that?" he inquired as he eyed the moldy object.

Sterling shrugged. "I suppose you could call it a token of our failure," he replied. "It's the sheath from the golden dagger. The Karnivans didn't take that."

Dathan, Sterling, and Lanna were more than a bit startled when Sir Keidric leaped to his feet, thrusting his trencher into the hands of the servant who hovered nearby. "Let me see it!"

Bewildered by the man's reaction, Sterling picked up the sheath and handed it to him. Sir Keidric eagerly examined the item. "Praise the name of Emmanuel!" he exulted. "Lad, your quest has not ended in failure—the golden dagger was not the item of value. This was!"

Sterling stared at the man. "I don't understand."

"The golden dagger that you carried for your father was not the real thing; it was not part of the crown jewels of Cheswold.

The dagger was a replica, a carefully crafted copy of the real dagger. Real gold, real jewels, aye, but still just a copy of the real thing. It was actually made as a decoy—the real dagger is safely hidden in a castle in Cheswold."

"But why is this sheath important?" Dathan interrupted. "It's just a dirty piece of moldy leather, and rather disgusting at that."

The man laughed. "Purposely. The sheath was made to be a foul, loathsome object that no one would want. We were hoping that if the Karnivans did get their hands on it, they would discard it. Apparently, the idea worked, and Sterling still has it with him as a result."

"But why is it important?"

"It's what's inside that matters," Sir Keidric replied cheerfully. He took his seat and received his trencher of food from the servant. "Allow me to tell you the whole story," he said.

He paused for a moment as if trying to decide where to begin his tale. "For the past several months, your father and I have been working closely with the Duke of Marden, planning a counter assault on the Karnivans to drive them from Cheswold once and for all."

Sterling leaned forward eagerly. "You know my father? Is he alive?"

"Aye, he is," Sir Keidric replied with a smile. "He is waiting for you at Lord Stratford's castle."

Dathan stared at the man. "Are you the Duke of Leeds?"

"I am. I am also Sterling's uncle."

Sterling's mouth actually fell open at this. "You are my...nay, that cannot be, sire."

The big man laughed. You don't remember me, do you, lad?"

"Nay, sire, I don't."

A look of amusement appeared on Sir Keidric's broad features. "Do you remember fishing in the moat of Windstone

Castle when you were just a little tyke, probably not more than three years old? You caught two little fish and a dead squirrel."

"Uncle Keith? You're Uncle Keith?"

"Well, actually, the name is Keidric, but you always called me 'Uncle Keith' even though your father worked to correct you."

"So that's why I've been dreaming about fishing in a castle moat," Sterling said. He stared at the duke. "But I haven't seen you in years, sire."

Sir Keidric looked uncomfortable. "Your father and I have been at odds until recently. The threat of the Karnivans has drawn us together again for a common cause." He stood up. "Rise, lad." When Sterling stood, the duke grabbed him and hugged him exuberantly. "It's good to see you again, lad."

Taking his seat, he placed the sheath across his knee and took a bite of venison. "Anyway, as I was saying, we have been planning a counter attack on the Karnivans to drive them from Cheswold forever. Lord Stratford has been helping us with men and supplies, smuggling them across the border from Ainranon. The Karnivans suspect something and have closed the border. Incidentally, had we not found you, you would have been captured at the border, no matter where you tried to cross. Emmanuel's name be praised that we found you when we did."

"Had we not followed the book, we never would have chosen this route," Dathan remarked.

"Aye. Be thankful that you followed the book."

Sterling frowned. "Why is the sheath so special? You said that the golden dagger was not the important item."

Sir Keidric did not reply. Instead, he took a knife and meticulously began to cut the stitching along the edge of the leather sheath. Dathan noticed that the Windstone knights immediately crowded in close and he knew that what they were about to see was of great significance. When the stitching was cut on three sides, the duke peeled back the leather, revealing a small, folded parchment. Carefully, painstakingly, the duke's big fingers unfolded the parchment and spread it upon his knee. The document was as thin as onion skin and when it was unfolded, the fugitives were surprised at how large a surface it covered. "This is the treasure you were transporting to Ainranon," Sir Keidric told them.

Dathan leaned closer. "What is it?"

"It's a map of Cheswold and certain regions of Karniva, showing the Karnivan war camps and listing troop concentrations," Sir Keidric replied, bending over the document and studying it with great interest. "It was smuggled to us by a Karnivan double agent who was gathering intelligence for us. The Karnivans are planning a massive assault on Cheswold at the end of this month; we plan to attack them first. By studying this map and learning exactly where Grimlor has his troops placed, we will know how to place our troops and most effectively plan our strategies."

He looked up from the map and a grin of delight spread across his features as he addressed the Windstone knights. "Gentlemen, the information here is more than we had hoped for. This gives us Karnivan troop rosters, battalion strengths, troop placements, and even shows Grimlor's plans for the coming battle. I doubt that Grimlor's generals have information this detailed about their own troops. This map is invaluable!"

He turned his attention to Sterling, Lanna, and Dathan. "You three have performed a valuable service to your country. Cheswold has three new heroes! The information you have provided will allow us to place our troops in the most strategic positions to defeat Grimlor and the Karnivans. Without this map, we would have been doomed to failure. On behalf of the entire nation of Cheswold, I thank you for your service and your sacrifice."

Carefully, the duke folded the map and placed it within his doublet and then retrieved his dinner from the servant. "Now, to see if we can get across the border and get this information to Lord Stratford."

Sterling looked up. "What are we to do, sire?"

"You're to accompany us, of course."

"And what are Dathan and I to do, sire?" Lanna asked fearfully.

Sir Keidric smiled. "You also are to accompany us to Lord Stratford's castle. There is a surprise awaiting you in Ainranon that will change your lives forever. What is about to take place will impact the lives of everyone in Cheswold, from the king down to the lowest peasant, and you two are major players in the drama."

A chill swept over Dathan as he heard the duke's words.

Chapter Eighteen

The Windstone knights rode two abreast as the entourage traveled silently through the dark hours of the morning. Sunrise was less than an hour away and Sir Keidric had stressed the importance of crossing the border while it was still dark. Faint streaks of pastel color painted the eastern skies, but the woods were dark and a thick mist obscured the trail.

The early morning air was chilly. Dathan clamped his elbows against his sides in an effort to stay warm. The entourage moved through the dark woods like a mouse hoping to avoid detection by a soaring hawk. The duke had warned them that the least little sound could give them away. Dathan's heart pounded and he knew that Lanna and Sterling were experiencing the same fears. He drew back on the reins, slowing his horse slightly so that Lanna's mount drew alongside his. She gave him a grateful smile.

The mountain grew steeper and the horses' breath hung in the air like gossamer phantoms as the animals labored up the trail. The sky was brightening noticeably as the entourage approached a narrow mountain pass. The inclines on each side of the pass were littered with thousands of huge, round boulders. Sir Keidric quietly called the riders to a halt. "Muffle the horses," he told the Windstone knights. "Their hooves will give us away on the flint trail." Dathan watched in fascination as the horsemen carefully wrapped their steeds' hooves in burlap mufflers to suppress any sounds on the trail. "Ride slowly," the duke cautioned. "We must tread softly here."

Dathan studied the slopes as the entourage rode silently through the pass, and he was just a bit worried. *If just one boulder should move,* he realized, *thousands would come crashing down upon us.* To his immense relief, the entourage passed through without incident.

On the far side of the pass, the mountain gave way to a series of gently rolling hills and just beyond them, a grassy valley. In the distance, purple mountains reached for an azure sky. Sir Keidric reined to a stop and sat tall in the saddle as he gazed over the panorama of great beauty. "Ainranon!" he said with a note of satisfaction in his voice. "Once we cross the valley, we will be beyond the reach of the dastardly Karnivans." Sir Lionel passed him and took the lead.

Just as Sir Lionel's powerful gray warhorse reached the bottom of the slope, a shrill cry split the silence of the morning and scores of Karnivan riders came sweeping down upon the entourage from a hidden draw. Sir Keidric took one look and immediately wheeled his mount around. "To the pass!" he shouted. "It's our only hope!"

The Windstone entourage turned their horses and raced for the mountain pass with the Karnivans hard on their heels. Dathan leaned forward in the saddle, urging his mount to greater speed. The gallant horse seemed to know that he was in a race against death as he galloped up the steep slope with flying mane and thundering hooves. Lanna's steed pulled up beside his and the two ran side by side with nostrils flared and necks straining. Dathan chanced a glance behind him and saw that the entourage had widened the gap between them and the Karnivans. Perhaps they would make it after all.

The Windstone entourage swept into the narrow pass. "Turn your mounts and quit yourselves like men!" Sir Keidric cried, and as one, the Windstone knights wheeled their mounts and turned to face the enemy. The pass was so narrow that three warhorses abreast completely filled the corridor. Sir Keidric had lessened the enemy's advantage of superior numbers by forcing them to fight in an arena where only a few would battle at a time. Dathan found that he, Lanna, and Sterling were positioned toward the rear of the entourage.

The Karnivan riders thundered into the pass and swept down upon the waiting Windstone men. Without slowing their mounts they crashed into the stationary block of riders. Horses screamed as they went down and suddenly, the battle was joined. Swords clashed. Karnivan knights streamed forward, clambering over fallen men and horses, scrambling under or around standing ones, and all the while screaming a furious battle cry that chilled the blood of those who heard it. The Windstone men fought valiantly, but they were slowly beaten back by the furious onslaught.

"Send petitions!" Dathan cried to Lanna and Sterling. "The battle is lost, but for the help of King Emmanuel!"

Snatching his book from within his tunic, he used his fingernail to scrawl a desperate message on the parchment:

"King Emmanuel,

Help, or all is lost!

Your son, Dathan."

Rolling the parchment tightly, he raised his right hand and released it, watching in desperate hope as the petition streaked over the trees of the forest. Petitions streaked from the hands of Sterling and Lanna at almost the same instant.

Sterling stood in the saddle and pointed. "Look! Uncle Keidric is hopelessly outnumbered!"

The tall nobleman's horse was gone and he was backed against the side of the pass, single-handedly battling four screaming Karnivans. Sir Keidric's sword flew swiftly, slashing here, parrying there as he battled for his life. "He'll be killed!" Lanna screamed.

A crash of thunder reverberated through the pass, so overwhelmingly powerful that every combatant paused and looked up in terror. The boulders on the ridges above the pass trembled as if about to fall. One boulder leaped from its place, hovered in midair for a fraction of a second, and then angled downward to strike two of the four Karnivans battling Sir Keidric. The impact crushed them to the ground like insects. A second boulder shot downward to crush the other two. Karnivans and Windstone men alike stood paralyzed, transfixed with horror.

And then, hundreds of boulders rose from their places, hovered briefly, and then pelted down upon the Karnivan forces like a veritable hailstorm of death. Knights and horses alike were crushed by the missiles, though not a single Windstone man was hit. With screams of terror, the remaining Karnivan troops turned and ran for their lives.

"It's as if invisible giants were hurling the boulders," Sterling said, staring in disbelief at the spectacle before them.

"King Emmanuel answered our petitions," Lanna replied with awe. "He's fighting for us."

"I think he sent the shining ones to battle for us," Dathan replied. "Though we could not see them, I think they were hurling the boulders. The book says that the shining ones are ministering spirits, sent forth to minister for them who shall be heirs to King Emmanuel."

"All praise to His Majesty, King Emmanuel!" Sir Keidric cried, raising his sword skyward. "But that he fought for us, we would all be dead men!"

Sir Lionel rode forward. "Sire, we have lost six men. Three others are sorely wounded."

"Lash the dead and injured to your saddles," the duke ordered. "We must make all haste to reach Ainranon as quickly as possible, lest the Karnivans regroup and return with reinforcements."

Within minutes, the Windstone men were ready to ride, though they struggled to clear the pass of dead men and horses just to get through. With somber faces and swords ready they rode the remaining few furlongs into Ainranon, but they encountered no opposition from the Karnivans.

Nearly an hour later they rode up the approach to a massive concentric castle situated high on a hill. As they neared the drawbridge, several knights rushed out to meet them. "Sir Keidric!" a stout nobleman called, "were you attacked?"

"Aye, Lord Stratford," the duke replied soberly, "and we lost several men. We have three wounded among us who need urgent care."

"It shall be done at once, sire," Lord Stratford replied. "Is the king safe?"

"Aye, that he is, Emmanuel be praised!"

What manner of greeting is that? Dathan wondered. *Is the king safe? How would Lord Keidric know whether or not the king is safe?*

The Windstone entourage rode across the drawbridge and into the castle barbican. They were immediately surrounded by knights and servants who took the dead and wounded away and then took charge of the horses. Sir Keidric approached Sterling. "Your father is away on a quest, but he will be back tomorrow. You will meet him then."

Sterling bowed. "I thank you, sire. I shall look forward to it."

Sir Keidric turned to Dathan. "Please, you and your sister are to come with me. Sterling too."

The three fugitives followed the duke through the inner gate, across the bailey, and into the great hall. Servants and castle staff were preparing the great hall for the breakfast meal, but three noblemen stood quietly talking at the far end of the hall. They looked up as Sir Keidric and his young charges approached.

Dathan recognized the nearest man and he stopped, too stunned to move or speak. His heart pounded. Could it be? It was impossible, but there was no mistaking the lively eyes or the welcoming smile. At last, he found his voice. "Papa!"

Chapter Nineteen

The Windstone knights were in a festive mood as they enjoyed the hospitality of Lord Stratford's table. The breakfast meal was the most bountiful meal that Dathan and Lanna had ever seen: thick slices of venison and pork roast, bacon and sausage and veal, poached eggs and muffins and fruits and jellies and... The servants kept returning to the table with platter after platter, each offering more interesting and appetizing than the last. Sterling and the twins ate and ate, grateful for the plenteous servings and the generosity of Lord Stratford and his staff.

Lord Stratford was seated at the head of the table with Sir Keidric on his immediate right and the twins' father on his left, and the three men were deep in discussions of troop placements and battle strategies as they planned the upcoming campaign against the Karnivans. Dathan was seated directly across from his father and as the meal progressed he found himself studying his every move. It had been so long...

"Papa," he said, during a lull in the conversation, "we never thought we would see you again! When we walked into the great hall and saw you standing there, we could hardly believe our eyes!"

Papa smiled and put an arm around Lanna, who was seated beside him. "You'll never know how grateful I am to see you safely here in Ainranon. Every day since we parted I have sent countless petitions to King Emmanuel on your behalf. His Majesty be praised, we are finally together again."

"Papa," Lanna asked fearfully, "will we have to go back to Windstone Castle and serve under Garven again? Isn't there some way you can buy us back from Lord Keidric?"

Her father smiled gently. "I know you don't understand all that transpired, but you do not really belong to Sir Keidric. You and Dathan are not servants, though you were led to believe that you were. I sent you to Windstone to place you under the protective custody of Sir Keidric while I was on a top secret quest, though it didn't work out quite the way I had planned, and for that I am truly sorry. I understand that this man Garven was quite hard on you, and again I am sorry."

"He wasn't just hard on us," Dathan interjected. "He was brutal."

His father nodded sympathetically. "I know that now. And I am sorry. Garven didn't know who you are."

"Who we are?" Dathan echoed. "What do you mean?"

"Well, first of all, there is something that both of you need to know, and I think this is as good a time as any to tell you. This will come as a shock, but I am not your father."

"Not our—" Dathan stopped, stunned by the words he had just heard. "But...then who..." His voice failed him.

"Papa!" Lanna cried. "Why do you say that?" Tears welled in her eyes. "We love you, Papa. Why do you say that you are not our father?"

The man struggled with his emotions. "I have raised you as if you were my own children and I have loved you as if you were my own," he said, and his voice was husky and low. "I have watched you grow and I have always thought of you as being mine, but I always knew that the day would come when you would be taken from me." He sighed. "Alas, that day is fast approaching, I fear."

"Taken from you? Oh, Papa, no!"

"If we are not your children," Dathan said slowly as his racing mind tried to digest the information he was hearing, "then who are we?"

"You were placed in my care when you were little tykes, barely two years old. My wife and I were given a charge to hide you until your sixteenth birthday."

"That's next month," Lanna declared.

"Aye, and no one knows that better than I. It will be a day of rejoicing for Cheswold, and yet in some ways, a day of great sorrow for me."

"Papa," Dathan said, "what are you talking about?"

He was interrupted by a roar of laughter from Lord Stratford, who was conversing with Lord Keidric. "So the Karnivans pursued the golden dagger, did they," Lord Stratford said, and another peal of laughter seemed to shake the great hall, "never knowing that in doing so, they were also pursuing the rightful king of Cheswold!" Lord Stratford was a huge man with a chest like a barrel, and when he laughed he shook the entire table. "Emmanuel be praised, they never knew that they were on the trail of the king!"

The twins turned and stared at Sterling. "We were traveling with royalty?" Dathan said in awe. "We ate and slept and traveled with a king and didn't even know it!"

Lanna's eyes grew wide. "You're...you're the king of Cheswold?"

"Nay, not Sterling," Lord Stratford corrected, and his laughter again filled the great hall. "Dathan!"

"Dathan?" Sterling stared at his friend in astonishment. "You...you and Lanna... you and Lanna are the missing prince and princess of Cheswold!"

"Prince and princess?" Dathan was overwhelmed. "How could we be the prince and princess of Cheswold? Sterling, that's impossible!"

Sterling continued to stare. "Dathan, you're Prince Eristan! That makes you the rightful king of Cheswold!"

"The king of—" Dathan choked on the words. "Now that is impossible!"

Sir Keidric looked at the twins' father. "Perhaps you should be the one to explain this, sire."

"Dathan and Lanna," Papa began, as he looked lovingly at the twins, "you grew up thinking that you were the son and daughter of a simple peasant carpenter, and that your mother died in childbirth. It is true that your mother died giving birth to you two, but what you didn't know is that your mother was Cordelia of Devonshire, Queen of Cheswold. Your father was King William."

"But—" Dathan started to protest, but Papa raised one hand. "Wait until you hear the story."

He took a drink from a tall goblet and then continued. "Three days after your second birthday, Cheswold was invaded by the Karnivans and King William's castle was placed under siege. My true name is Reginald of Orwyn. I was the castle constable, in charge of the king's knights and the castle defenses, yet your father ordered my wife and me to flee the castle to protect you. Though his castle was under siege and the throne was in jeopardy, his first thoughts were for your welfare. Under cover of night, we took you and fled the castle through a secret underground tunnel."

He cleared his throat and continued. "Your father was killed in the ensuing battle and the crown jewels were lost to the

Karnivans, save for the golden dagger. I fled to a shire far from the castle, assumed the name of Willis, and became a carpenter. We also changed your names to protect your identity. My wife died of consumption the next year and I was left to raise you by myself. No one in all Cheswold knew where the royal twins were taken, or whether or not they are still alive, but next month all of Cheswold shall learn who you are. Dathan, your real name is Eristan, and you are heir to the throne of Cheswold."

"But—but what about King Vladimir?"

"When the Karnivans were routed from Cheswold, Vladimir became the king. King Vladimir is actually just a regent, placed on the throne to rule Cheswold until you reach your sixteenth birthday, at which time you will take the throne and he will step down."

Dathan shook his head. "This is all so confusing. This is... this is unbelievable!"

Papa laughed. "I'm sure it is. It's hard to go from being a commoner to being the king in a moment's time. That's enough to befuddle any man."

"But I'm not ready to be king! And what about the Karns? I don't know how to battle against them!"

"You'll have a cabinet of some of the most capable generals in all Terrestria," Sir Keidric said gently. "We're with you all the way, lad, uh... Your Majesty! We love Cheswold as much as you do, and we'll help you in every way we can."

"But I am just a youth," Dathan protested. "I'm not ready to rule an entire nation!"

"I'd like to try," Sterling remarked.

"Do you think you're capable of being king, lad?" Sir Keidric fixed Sterling with a stern gaze.

Sterling lowered his eyes. "Nay, sire."

"What about the Karns?" Dathan asked again. "I'm not capable of leading Cheswold against them. I am but a youth. I have no military experience."

"You are King Eristan, the rightful king of Cheswold," Reginald said quietly but firmly. "It is only right that you take the throne. You will have the finest counselors in Terrestria at your disposal, and you have King Emmanuel's book to guide you. Though it is true that you have no military experience, you can be assured of success if you simply follow the book. Son, you are my king, King Eristan of Cheswold."

Eristan hesitated. He was silent for several long moments. At last, he spoke. "I will take the throne on one condition."

"Name it, Your Majesty." The men around the table waited breathlessly for his words.

Eristan turned to Sir Reginald. "You must continue to be my father. You are the wisest man I have ever known, and I am proud to be called your son. I will take the throne only if Lanna and I may continue to call you 'Papa' and we may continue to be 'Dathan' and 'Lanna.' We cannot lose you as our father."

Sir Reginald nodded. "As you wish, Dathan. Next month shall be your coronation day, and you shall take the throne as Eristan, King of Cheswold. I will be honored to be known as your father."

Eristan looked at his sister. "Can you believe what we have just heard in the last few minutes? This is incredible!"

Lanna shook her head and laughed. "I can't believe that my twin brother is going to be the king of Cheswold! If you are the king, what does that make me?"

"You are Princess Cordelia, the princess of Cheswold, dear," Sir Reginald told her. "The people of Cheswold will come to love you, just as they will love King Eristan."

"Cordelia?" the princess echoed. "I have the same name as my mother?"

"She gave you her name when she realized that she was dying," Sir Reginald said quietly.

Silence reigned at the table as the young prince and princess struggled to assimilate the wealth of information they had just been handed. Finally, Eristan looked teasingly at his sister. "It's hard to believe that I will soon be the King of Cheswold," he said with a grin, "but it's even harder to think of you as a princess!"

Sir Reginald laughed.

A look of delight spread across Princess Cordelia's face. "I just thought of something, Dathan, uh, King Eristan. I'd like to see Garven's face when he learns that you are the king of Cheswold. You can punish him for what he did to us. You can have him publicly flogged!"

"Why would I do that?" Eristan asked quietly.

"Because of what he did to us," Cordelia responded.

Eristan shook his head. "I must confess that the idea appeals to me because of the humiliation and pain he inflicted upon us. But as the King of Cheswold, I cannot do what I want to do; I must allow King Emmanuel's book to guide me in every decision that I make. Though I would like to pay Garven back for what he did to us, I must follow the book, and nowhere does it tell me to inflict pain upon Graven because he inflicted pain upon us.

"Aye, he will stand before me to answer for what he has done, but if I find in him a repentant spirit, I will forgive him, for thus the book commands."

"Spoken like a true king, Your Majesty," Sir Reginald said. "May your reign be crowned with success, may King Emmanuel protect and guide you, and may the Karnivans be smitten before you."

Prince Eristan smiled. "Thank you, Papa. The battle for Cheswold will be long and hard, of this I am certain, but with King Emmanuel's hand upon us we shall prevail, and the Karnivans shall be driven from Cheswold forever."

If your heart has been touched by the Terrestria series, we encourage you to...

invite others to visit Terrestria.

If you've read the Terrestria books you're already realized that they were written to honor the Lord Jesus Christ and to draw young people and their parents into a close relationship with Him.

Readers whose hearts have been touched by the Terrestria stories have asked what they can do to help get the books in the hands of others and give the series the widest circulation possible. In a culture saturated with advertising, word of mouth remains the best and most effective means of spreading the word. Here's what you can do to help share the books with others...

- Give Terrestria books to friends and family members as gifts. If you cannot afford to give away entire sets, choose the single book that impacted you in the greatest way and give that one book.
- Donate books to your local school libraries and public libraries in order to place the Gospel into the public forum and perhaps reach young people who do not otherwise have access to the Gospel message. Hardbound editions of The Terrestria Chronicles are available in complete sets; single hardbound copies of Book 1 are also available.
- If you have a web site or blog, consider mentioning the books and how they have touched your life. Recommend that others read the books and link to www.TalesOfCastles.com.
- Write book reviews for your local paper, homeschool or parents' magazines, or your favorite web sites. Don't

give away the plots but tell just enough to whet the appetites of your readers.

- Contact ministries that specialize in family issues or provide parenting resources and recommend that they review the books in their magazines or communications. You might even suggest that they carry the series. Often these ministries will give more consideration to the requests of their listeners than the press releases and reviews from publishing houses.
- Contact bookstores and distributors and recommend that they consider the Terrestria series. One large discount distributor began to carry the series after they were contacted by an enthusiastic homeschool family.
- Donate a set of books to a prison, juvenile center, or rehabilitation home where the residents might be helped by the stories and the messages they contain.
- Talk about the books on email lists, parenting or homeschooling forums and other places where you interact with others on the Internet. Homeschool families in particular are looking for conservative, Christ-honoring reading materials for their families. One missionary mom in Fiji recommended the series on a mother's list; two weeks later another mom on the same list echoed the recommendation, resulting in hundreds of Terrestria books going into the homes of eager families.
- Introduce the Terrestria series to friends at church and at school. If your children attend private school, suggest to the administration that they conduct a Terrestria book fair to get the books into the hands of the students. One teacher in Pennsylvania reads *The Crown of Kuros* to his fifth grade class every year. A Canadian pastor has sold

or given away more than two hundred complete sets to his congregation and to fellow pastors.

- Pray that God will use the series in a great way to touch hearts and change lives. Pray that He will direct and that Christ will be glorified as future Terrestria books are written.

www.TalesOfCastles.com